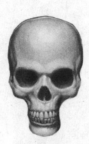

D0047510

RETURN TO FEAR STREET

YOU MAY NOW
KILL
THE BRIDE

R.L. STINE

HARPERTEEN
An Imprint of HarperCollinsPublishers

HarperTeen is an imprint of HarperCollins Publishers.

You May Now Kill the Bride
Copyright © 2018 by Parachute Publishing, LLC

Library of Congress Control Number: 2017962479
ISBN 978-0-06-269425-6

Typography by Jenna Stempel-Lobell
18 19 20 21 22 PC/LSCH 10 9 8 7 6 5 4 3 2 1
❖
First Edition

Dedicated to my bride who, I hope, isn't related to the Fears

PART ONE

1923

ONE

Ruth-Ann Fear remembered the feel of hands wrapping around her neck from behind. She remembered the startling pressure and how warm the hands were—warm and damp.

She remembered the leap her heart made, the gasp that escaped her throat. The fingers tightening until she struggled for breath.

With a hard twist of her body, she spun around—and stared into Peter Goodman's eyes. She made another sound, this time a cry of recognition.

He lowered his hands, the fingers sliding gently now, tracing a damp path along her throat. His touch now tender. Still not breathing, Ruth-Ann watched a smile form on his lips.

"Did I startle you?" His grin grew wider. He knew the answer.

Why did Peter enjoy scaring her, sneaking up on her, catching her off guard? Was it just another boy thing, having to prove himself superior? Showing Ruth-Ann who was in charge?

She took both of his hands in hers. "I knew it was you," she lied. She tugged him close and pressed her mouth against his. An awkward kiss. He was still enjoying his little prank.

He kissed her again. Ruth-Ann pushed him back with both hands on the lapels of his dark suit jacket. "Do you like my dress?" She stuck out both arms, modeling it for him. It was pale blue, shiny as silk, a wide bow tied at the waist, the skirt falling to her ankles.

His eyes moved up and down. "It's the cat's whiskers, Ruth-Ann. What did your mum and dad say about your haircut?"

Her eyes flashed. "They loved it."

"Go chase yourself!" he exclaimed. "Even *you* can't keep a straight face when you say that."

She laughed. "Okay. The truth. They hated it. They said, 'Just because a lot of foolish, misguided young women are cutting their hair into short bobs, why do you have to follow them?'"

"Good question," Peter muttered.

Ruth-Ann raised her pale blue cap and brushed her short, coppery hair with one hand. "Why? You think I look like a boy?"

Peter's cheeks turned pink. "Of course not." He leaned forward and kissed her again.

"Actually, Mum and Dad didn't make much of a fuss. That's because it was *me* with the bobbed hair. If it was Rebecca, they would have gone blooey. At least they would have canceled this birthday party."

Peter raised a finger to her lips. "Stop, Ruth-Ann. You're always saying how they like Rebecca better than you—"

She pushed his finger away. "You know it's the truth. Do you know the first thing Mum said when she saw my new haircut? She said, 'Don't worry. It will grow back.'"

Peter started to laugh but stopped when a car horn honked. They both turned to see a bright red roadster rumble up the gravel drive.

Two girls in long party dresses hurried across the grass to greet the car. On the terrace, two maids in black-and-white uniforms were setting down trays of drinking glasses.

Peter turned away from Ruth-Ann and started toward the house. She grabbed his hand. "Peter, where are you going?"

"Inside," he replied. "I want to try your father's—"

"—Radio set." She finished the sentence for him. It was maybe the only thing Peter Goodman and Randolph Fear had in common. They both loved to spend hours tuning in distant radio stations on Mr. Fear's radio receiver.

"No," Ruth-Ann insisted. "You have to help me get through Rebecca's birthday party." She tugged him toward the lawn. "Come say hello to Mum and Dad."

"Right now?" Peter said. He shrugged. "Why? They don't like me anyway."

"Please. They think you're the bee's knees." Ruth-Ann knew she was lying. Her parents didn't like Peter at all.

"The boy has no gumption." That's what her father had said. "Why doesn't he ever look me in the eye? Is he hiding something? He talks into his chin. I can't hear a word he mumbles."

But Peter was good enough for Ruth-Ann. If Peter were dating Rebecca, her parents would demand that President Harding call out the army to chase him off. Or they would put Rebecca on the next passenger ship to Europe to break them up.

Rebecca was the princess. Randolph Fear even called her that. "Princess."

Her parents had little to say about Peter dating Ruth-Ann, and she was glad. She needed something or some*one* to be hers and hers alone, and Peter fit the bill.

He wasn't the most exciting guy in Shadyside, or the best-looking. In fact, with his chubby cheeks and round black-framed glasses, his straight brown hair down over his forehead, he looked a lot like an owl.

Peter wasn't the funniest, or the sharpest dresser. His family wasn't rich or important. He didn't have to be any of those things to make Ruth-Ann happy. And she realized that Peter was one of the few people who *did* make her feel happy, not in second place, not like Rebecca Fear's little sister.

Peter was halfway to the house. "You can't stay in there the whole time," Ruth-Ann called to him. "You have to come out and be social. You have to come out when lunch is served. *Do you hear me?*"

He turned back and gave her a little wave of one hand. His glasses caught the sunlight and made it look as if his face was lighting up.

She heard her mother shouting. "Ruth-Ann? Where are you? The Grainers are here. Ruth-Ann?"

But she stood and watched Peter, watched him until he disappeared behind the terrace door.

Peter. Peter. Peter . . .

She had no idea how soon he would betray her.

TWO

One year later, Ruth-Ann had many lingering memories of Rebecca's birthday party. She remembered her talk with Peter. Remembered the excitement of kissing him. And after that . . . she remembered the yellow sky.

She could picture their sloping lawn . . . the blue and white balloons that bobbed and swayed in a warm, gentle breeze . . . the pots of daffodils on every table, Rebecca's favorite flower. No clouds, but the sky was low and the color of buttermilk, a fantasy sky.

And everything seemed perfect, Ruth-Ann remembered. She could still hear the soft voices and laughter, and see Rebecca's girlfriends in their long, colorful silk dresses and feathery, flowery hats. The boys in their light suits, their Oxfords shined, their shirt collars open to the sunlight.

She remembered Jonny Penderman rolling up the gravel driveway in that pale blue touring car, the sides and the wheels blue as a bird's egg. Kids jumped on the running boards on both sides of the car and hung on while Jonny made the tires spin over the gravel.

Ruth-Ann's father appeared and squinted at her through his round eyeglasses. Randolph Fear was a short man, a bit overweight, his dark pinstripe suit strained at the waist, his stiff white collar a little too tight.

He pointed to the car. "Look at that jalopy. That boy should be ashamed to drive up in a bus like that."

Ruth-Ann rolled her eyes. "Funny, Dad."

Randolph shook his head. "That car must cost a heap of simoleons. Where does that Penderman boy get the money to own a car like that?"

Simoleons? Her father prided himself on his knowledge of the current slang. He thought he could impress his two daughters by "being hip to their jive." But he usually embarrassed them and got things completely wrong.

"It's Jonny's father's car," Ruth-Ann said, moving toward the driveway.

Randolph followed beside her. "Didn't that boy carry a torch for you for a while?"

Ruth-Ann frowned. "He's Rebecca's friend, Dad." *Everyone here is Rebecca's friend*, she thought, with only a little bitterness. *Everyone loves Rebecca.*

She watched her sister flirt with Jonny Penderman. He pulled open the car door for Rebecca, and she slid gracefully behind the wheel, tucking her long skirt under her. A circle of kids had gathered to admire the long blue car.

"I can get seven passengers in here. Easy," Jonny was saying as Ruth-Ann drew near. "It rides like a dream. And yesterday, I was out past the north farms—no one in sight for miles—and I got her up to forty miles an hour."

Some guys laughed. "That's hooey."

"Tell us another one."

"Are you going to enter it in a race?"

Jonny raised his right hand. "I swear. The car was rattling like crazy. I was bouncing so hard, my head kept bumping the roof. I glanced down at the meter, and it said forty."

More hoots and laughter.

"I believe you, Jonny," Rebecca said from the driver's seat. "Can I drive it?"

"Do you have a driver's license?"

"No. Do you need a license to drive a car? Nerts to that!"

She slid out of the car and rearranged her red hat over her blond hair.

"I'm going to drive it to New York City," Jonny announced. "Anyone want to come with me?"

"I do!" Ruth-Ann cried. She glimpsed her father frowning at her. She knew he'd never allow either of his daughters to go on a trip like that. Too far and too dangerous.

"Why are you driving to New York?" Rebecca's tall blond lookalike friend, Lily Wayne, asked.

"To see the new baseball stadium," Jonny answered. "Yankee Stadium. They don't share with the Giants anymore. They opened it last week against the Red Sox."

Ruth-Ann knew that Jonny was a big baseball fan. And so were a lot of the other guys, who loudly begged him to take them along.

She had to laugh. Who said Jonny's dad would allow Jonny to take this beautiful new touring car that far? Jonny was a great guy, a lot of fun, but he wasn't the most responsible kid in the world.

She smiled. Jonny's dad had let him drive another brand-new roadster when he was fifteen—and he rode over a milkman's horse!

Now, one year later, a year after that happy birthday

party, Ruth-Ann remembered the pale blue car under the yellow sky. And the deep ruby red of Rebecca's dress, swirling around her as she moved from guest to guest. Rebecca the smiling host, so warm and winning.

Only the best for Rebecca. Ruth-Ann knew that dress cost almost twenty dollars. It was silk crepe, after all, with those beautiful pleats down the skirt to her ankles.

Ruth-Ann remembered everything about Rebecca that day. Rebecca's red velvet hat with the single feather standing from the back like a sword. The suede Indian moccasins she wore. Her blue eyes darting from guest to guest.

The way she hurried to greet Nelson Swift. The confident way she took Nelson's arm and guided him to the drinks table, chattering like a happy little sparrow all the way.

Ruth-Ann watched them at the party, watched Nelson's slicked-down black hair parted so perfectly in the middle of his tanned forehead. His pale green eyes, fox eyes. His toothy smile that never seemed real. His single-breasted black suit fitted so perfectly.

Watching him move in and out of the sunlight, crystal glass sparkling in his raised hand, smile plastered in place. His perfect posture. His perfect *everything*.

And Ruth-Ann asked herself: *Is Rebecca really going to marry Nelson Swift?*

That was her father's fantasy. But it couldn't possibly be Rebecca's, could it?

If only the sisters had been closer, they could discuss such things. Rebecca was only four years older than Ruth-Ann. They pretended to be close. But they never spoke of personal things, of the things dear to their hearts, the things that really mattered. Were there such wide gaps in other families, too?

Questions. So many questions.

Now it was a year since the party, and Rebecca's wedding was near. Days away. But Ruth-Ann preferred to linger in the past. To think about the party. The colors. The smiles. The jokes and laughter. Rebecca and her friends. Jonny and his touring car. Nelson and his grip on Rebecca's arm.

Peter . . . Oh, Peter. Peter, why?

THREE

The trouble didn't start until a few weeks after the party. All had agreed the party had been a big success.

It seemed to put Rebecca in a rare good mood. Several times, Ruth-Ann caught her humming to herself. And once, she peeked into Rebecca's room and saw her singing and practicing a wild new dance, some sort of jazz step with her arms shooting above her head and her shoes tapping the floor.

Rebecca froze when she saw Ruth-Ann peering in at her. Ruth-Ann braced for an angry tirade. Usually, Rebecca didn't like to be spied on.

But, to Ruth-Ann's surprise, Rebecca smiled at her and waved her into the room. "It's a new step I learned at the Hot Bunny Club with Nelson. Want me to teach you?"

Ruth-Ann could feel herself blushing. "You know how clumsy I am."

But Rebecca insisted. They stumbled through the dance step a few times, laughing and bumping into each other. For once, Rebecca didn't get frustrated. She kept patiently urging Ruth-Ann, who was as clumsy as she claimed, to try it again.

We're actually having fun together, Ruth-Ann thought.

Ruth-Ann's shoes tapped the floor. She flung her hands up—and lost her balance, and the two sisters ended up laughing in a tangled heap on the carpet. "Maybe we should try a waltz," Rebecca said.

She dragged Ruth-Ann to her feet. "Nelson got two tickets to see the Paul Whiteman band on Saturday at the Palladium," she said. She winked. "He can be useful."

She pulled Ruth-Ann to her dressing table. "Come help me put up my hair."

What an odd thing to say, Ruth-Ann thought. *He can be* useful?

Rebecca sat down in front of the tall mahogany mirror and opened a quilted box of hairpins. "My hair is so long and heavy, I feel like I'm wearing a blanket on my head."

Ruth-Ann shook her head quickly from side to side to make her short hair flare out. "You spend hours putting your hair up, bringing it down, brushing it out. I just give my head a shake, and I'm ready to go."

Rebecca rolled her eyes. "I'd *love* to give your head a shake."

They both laughed.

Their faces were side by side in the mirror. Ruth-Ann gazed at their reflection as if seeing them for the first time. She wasn't a golden-haired, blue-eyed princess like Rebecca. But she knew she wasn't bad-looking.

She had warm, wide brown eyes and a winning smile. Her parents were always urging her to smile more often, but it didn't come naturally.

Her hair was coppery, darker than Rebecca's. Her nose wasn't as graceful as her sister's. And she had a tiny dimple in her chin that she hated.

I'm not as pretty as she is, Ruth-Ann thought. *But I'm more interesting.*

Was that really true?

Rebecca was twenty-one, and a good life was pretty much set out for her. Randolph Fear had secured her an apprentice job at Mrs. Paul's, the milliner shop in town. Rebecca was artistic, and she wanted to be a designer of ladies' hats.

Mrs. Paul said she showed a wonderful flair for it. She said she would help Rebecca submit her designs to a hatmaker in New York.

And then there was Nelson.

True, Dad had picked Nelson out for Rebecca. Nelson worked at Mr. Fear's investment firm. The stock market was booming in 1923, and Nelson was the company's biggest money earner.

Nelson was big and boyish and boastful, loud and sometimes a little vulgar. He liked to laugh a lot. Ruth-Ann knew that Rebecca hated the way he was always slapping people on the back or poking a finger on their chest as he spoke to them.

He's like a warm, friendly animal, Ruth-Ann thought when Dad brought him to dinner that night. *He's so eager to please, he'll lick your face to make you like him. A big, warm puppy dog.*

He was only twenty-one, the same age as Rebecca. But he smoked cigars and wore dark pinstripe suits from New York, and acted like a tycoon.

Mr. Fear had invited Nelson home to dinner and

practically thrust Rebecca and him into each other's laps! Most of the time, Rebecca seemed happy with Nelson. She liked dancing and going to the new jazz clubs on the other side of town.

But Ruth-Ann could never tell if Rebecca was serious about him. Standing behind her sister at the mirror, their faces looming so close together in the reflection, Ruth-Ann worked up her courage. Maybe she and Rebecca could have a real sister-to-sister talk.

"You and Nelson—" she started.

But Rebecca cut her off. "I think Peter is too old for you," she said.

Ruth-Ann blinked. She had to steady herself. It was so unexpected.

"Peter is my age," Rebecca said, eyes straight ahead into the mirror. "You're still in high school."

"Only for a few months," Ruth-Ann snapped. Her surprise began to turn into anger. *Why is Rebecca saying this?*

She started to pin a rolled-up strand of Rebecca's hair. But her hand slipped and the pin jabbed the back of her sister's neck.

"Ow!" Rebecca screamed and spun toward Ruth-Ann. "You don't have to attack me. I'm not a pincushion!"

She rubbed the back of her neck. "That was vicious, Ruth-Ann. I was just trying to help you."

Ruth-Ann took a step back. "It—it was an accident," she stammered. "Really, Rebecca. My hand slipped."

"I'm your big sister," Rebecca said, softening her tone. "I know you and I aren't exactly best pals. But I care about you. And I think you're heading for trouble with Peter."

Ruth-Ann stood with her mouth open. She couldn't shake off the shock of her sister's words. "Peter and I—"

Rebecca turned back to the mirror, but her eyes remained on Ruth-Ann. "He's a Victrola salesman," she said with a sneer. "Where is *that* going to lead?"

"He—he's learning how to repair Victrolas as well," Ruth-Ann said. "Peter is very mechanical. He is fascinated by record players and radio receivers."

"No one else is," Rebecca replied. "Do you really think people are going to put those things in their homes and stand around listening to them?"

"Well . . ."

"He's so immature," Rebecca said, rolling her eyes. "I'll bet he reads all those H. G. Wells novels about time machines. Does Peter want to sell time machines, too, Ruth-Ann?"

"Now you're just being cruel," Ruth-Ann said, lowering her voice to a whisper. She felt her anger rise in her chest. "I—I don't know why you're saying these things."

"I told you. I care about you."

"Peter and I have good times together," Ruth-Ann said. "We laugh a lot. We enjoy being with each other. We understand each other."

"That's wonderful," Rebecca said sarcastically. "But—"

"He works hard," Ruth-Ann continued. "He wants to be a success. And we do things together when he's not working. We take long bike rides up on the River Ridge. We have picnics in Shadyside Park . . ."

Rebecca slammed a fist on the dressing table. The box of hairpins jumped. "Ruth-Ann, you need a *future*. You're graduating from high school next month. You have no plans. What are you going to do with your life? You need a husband, a man to take care of you. Not a boy who spends all his time trying to hear voices on the radio waves."

Ruth-Ann realized her hands were balled into tight fists. She uncoiled her hands and took a deep breath. "So is that why you're so attached to Nelson? You need a man to take care of you?"

"Nelson is Nelson," Rebecca said. She sighed. "He is okay sometimes. But he can be a bear."

Ruth-Ann squinted at her sister's reflection. "A bear? What does that mean?"

Rebecca clawed the air with her hands and uttered a low animal growl. Like a bear growl.

"Would you care to explain?" Ruth-Ann urged.

Rebecca sighed. She waved a hand at the mirror. "Go away, Ruth-Ann. Just scram. I can do my own hair."

Ruth-Ann gasped. *She really thinks she can give me a royal proclamation about Peter. Then send me on my way. Am I supposed to bow and say thank you?*

"Nice talking to you, Rebecca," Ruth-Ann murmured. She spun away from the mirror and, taking long, heavy strides, stormed out of her sister's room.

The shock of Rebecca's sudden attack on Peter had Ruth-Ann dizzy and off balance. She bumped the wall as she turned into the hallway, stopped, and shut her eyes, waiting for the dizziness to fade.

Rebecca must have been thinking about this for a long time, Ruth-Ann thought. *She was waiting to ambush me. But—why?*

Anger battled with her confusion. The one time she thought she was getting close enough to her sister to have a real, honest conversation, Rebecca hit her with a sneak attack.

Ruth-Ann realized she had clenched her teeth. Her jaw started to ache. She took a deep breath. She decided not to go to her room across the hall.

Instead, she took hurried steps to the end of the hallway. She turned at a closed door and grabbed the brass knob. She twisted and pulled, and in a few seconds slipped into the narrow stairway that led up to the attic she had discovered years ago.

Ruth-Ann was careful to close the door behind her. The stairway didn't lead to the attic everyone used. The stairs to that attic—cluttered with old furniture and clothing, cartons and crates of the discarded and forgotten—were at the other end of the house.

This narrow stairway, steep and creaky, climbed to a separate room, a windowless room that sunshine could never invade, a room that only Ruth-Ann used, that only Ruth-Ann knew about.

A room of secrets.

Her heart was racing when she reached the top of the stairs and stepped into the warm darkness of the tiny space. Her hand found the kerosene candlelighter where she had left it and, a few seconds later, three flickering flames at the tops of long, slender candles lit the room.

Ruth-Ann waited for her eyes to adjust to the darkness. The candle flames danced and sent shadows pulsing over the low ceiling. The air was warm and dry and smelled of sharp spices, the spices Ruth-Ann used to cast her spells.

It was time to cast another.

FOUR

The little attic room was bare, except for the floor-to-ceiling bookshelves on three walls. The shelves sagged, loaded down with ancient, dust-covered volumes, the covers worn and faded. One book was open on the wood floor, resting between a circle of ten black candles.

Ruth-Ann's anger had faded now, replaced by the excitement this room always brought. The excitement of delving into mysteries, dark mysteries that went beyond science, beyond human understanding.

Ruth-Ann's secret was her ability to cast spells, and part of the excitement came from knowing that only she was capable of performing this magic. The books of sorcery, of evil chants and curses and strange powers, must have been in her family for generations.

Did her parents even know this tiny attic room existed? They had inherited the house after her grandparents died, and yet this room remained untouched. Did they ever explore up here? Did they know the powers the Fears could possess if they used the instructions in these old books?

Ruth-Ann had discovered the room by accident one afternoon when she was seven years old. An intense game of hide-and-seek led to her running to the end of the hall. She could hear her friends' approaching footsteps and knew she had only seconds to hide.

The narrow door caught her eye. Seconds later, she was up in the hidden attic, gasping for breath, holding on to the wall, leaning over the stairway and listening for her pursuers.

They didn't come. She heard shouts and more running footsteps. But no one tried the door. No one found her. She began to breathe easy. This was her secret place, she realized. Her secret hiding place from the world.

Years later, she had the curiosity to pull out some of the old books on the shelves, dust them off, and read what they offered.

The history of her family was up here. Did her parents even know any of it? Did they know about the Fears' archenemies, the Goode Family? Ruth-Ann had never heard anyone mention the Goodes.

The two families had hated each other since the early days of this country. Since Colonial days. Since the burning of witches and lives ruled by all kinds of dark superstitions.

Ruth-Ann read of the hatred, of the curses the two families cast on each other, of the *murders* that were carried out, all in the name of the ancient family rivalry.

The stories made her feel cold all over. *The history of my family is so strange and so evil*, she thought. And that was *before* she began to comb through the spell books, before she learned of the sorcery that her family had learned, powers that even she could master with enough practice and study.

She read the spells. She memorized some of them. She practiced a few harmless ones just to see if they would work. She made rabbits dance in a circle in her backyard. She made squirrels chase a dog down the street.

She didn't try a serious spell until her sixteenth birthday.

The day was lonely with few friends. Ruth-Ann spent the day envying Rebecca with her easy grace and all her many admirers. Rebecca, so popular. So bubbling and happy. The princess who seldom allowed Ruth-Ann to even stand in her shadow.

Yes, it was envy that propelled Ruth-Ann. Envy that drove her to the ancient spell books and the black candles and the rituals she needed to get what she wanted.

It was only then that Ruth-Ann decided she needed a boyfriend. And she knew how to get one. It was 1922, after all, and everything was modern. Everyone was modern. Including the girls.

She picked Peter Goodman. She had been attracted to him at school. All the girls talked and giggled and whispered about their "crushes." Maybe Ruth-Ann had a crush on Peter.

She didn't know if he liked *her* or not. It didn't really matter. Ruth-Ann's summoning spell was powerful and inescapable. Once she had chosen Peter, he was hers. And she knew the sorcery to keep him as long as she wanted.

Two weeks after Rebecca's birthday party, Ruth-Ann decided she wanted him *now*.

To defy Rebecca, yes. Rebecca and her unwanted advice to say good-bye to Peter.

Rebecca had no clue as to who had the real power in the family. Ruth-Ann planned to keep it that way. How wonderful to perform miracles behind a cloak of shadows. How pleasing to control people without their knowledge, to manipulate them with just candlelight and words and songs.

And now she wanted Peter to arrive. She wanted her boyfriend, the only boyfriend she had ever had. "I want you here now, Peter," she murmured, lighting the ten black candles one by one.

She stood in the center of the circle, in the pale white glow of the candlelight, and began to remove her clothes. She pulled off the frilly blouse and tossed it against the wall. Her skirt came off next, and then the petticoats. Her undergarments flew against the wall.

And Ruth-Ann stood naked in the shadowy light from the darting, swaying flames all around her. She raised her arms like bird wings, as if flying free. And she began to dance.

A delicate dance at first, on tiptoe, with her hands swaying slow and high above her head. She shook out her short hair and kept her hands high, her bare feet tapping the warm wooden floor. And she began to sing. A soft, tender song of words in a strange language, a song from the book at her feet.

Ruth-Ann sang and did her slow, sinuous dance, her body warm from the candlelight, her skin shadowy in the darting flames and the wisps of black smoke from the points of the flames. The wisps of her dark magic.

She sang the words in a whispery voice. Her skin tingling, so free and light without clothes that she felt she could fly.

And when the spell was cast, she dressed quickly. She snuffed out the candles, and shook out her hair one more time. Then she hurried downstairs, peeking into the hall, making sure no one could see where she was coming from.

She had to wait only a few minutes.

When the front doorbell rang, her mother started to the door. But Ruth-Ann stopped her halfway. "Don't bother, Mum," she said. "It's for me."

FIVE

A week later, Ruth-Ann and Peter sat close together on the brown leather couch in the sitting room. Her mother had been in the chair across from them, knitting a scarf. When she got up to leave, Ruth-Ann leaned her cheek toward Peter for a kiss.

Peter didn't seem to take the hint. He kept talking about the article he had read in a science magazine. The article said that the wireless would replace all the pianos in living rooms across the nation.

"People will listen to music from far away," Peter said. "They will no longer have to make their own." He smiled at her. "That could be very bad for the people who print sheet music," he said.

Ruth-Ann rolled her eyes. "What makes you think people will want to listen to all the scratchy whistling and static?"

"They'll fix all that," Peter said. "The article said it will sound like an orchestra is right in your living room."

Again, Ruth-Ann brought her face an inch from his. "What do I have to do to get a kiss?"

He gave her a peck on the cheek. Disappointed, she blew on his glasses, steaming up both sides.

He uttered an uncomfortable laugh and drew away from her.

"What's wrong?" she demanded. He was definitely acting nervous today. Chattering on about a magazine article . . . refusing to kiss her . . .

Peter shrugged.

She playfully flipped his necktie over the shoulder of his sports jacket. "Aren't you feeling well?"

A burst of laughter from the kitchen interrupted Peter's reply.

"Who's in there?" he asked.

"Rebecca and three of her friends," Ruth-Ann replied. "They're teaching each other how to make Apple Brown Betty."

Peter jumped to his feet. "Apple Brown Betty? Hot diggety. Can we see how they are doing?"

Ruth-Ann squinted at him. "Are you *sure* you're feeling okay? You hate talking with Rebecca and her friends. You said they were shallow, remember?"

"That's before there was Apple Brown Betty involved," he replied. He grabbed her hands and tugged her up from the couch. "Besides, you're always telling me to be more social."

"Not with Rebecca and her crowd," Ruth-Ann muttered.

Ever since Rebecca's attack on Peter, the two sisters barely spoke. They were like two icebergs passing in the ocean. Ruth-Ann didn't think she could *ever* forgive her sister for that outburst.

She'd spent hours trying to figure out what caused it. But she still hadn't thought of a good reason behind her sister's attack.

Rebecca was pretending she cares about me. But she was only being vicious.

And now here was Peter, eager to join Rebecca in the kitchen. This was not like him at all. "I can bake things, too," Ruth-Ann said. "Why don't we wait till they're finished and—"

But he was already at the kitchen door, greeting everyone.

If I told him what Rebecca said about him last week,

Peter would forget about that Apple Brown Betty.

And then she thought, *Do I have to cast a spell to get him to act normally again? Do I have to cast a spell to get him to kiss me?*

A few seconds later, the girls were all gathered around the counter, and Peter was slicing apples, and measuring out the cinnamon, laughing and chatting, suddenly at ease and the life of the party.

Rebecca's best friend, Lily Wayne, was there with a long white apron over her flowery yellow dress. And Jonny Penderman was teasing her, poking her with a spatula, making her squeal each time.

Peter grinned at Jonny and pointed. "Jonny, how did you get flour on your nose?"

Jonny grinned back. "It was easy." He reached across the counter and poked his finger deep into the bag of flour. Then he rubbed his finger on Peter's nose, leaving a nice white smear.

"Hey—!" Peter uttered a cry. He picked up the flour bag, and pulled his arm back as if to heave it at Jonny. Jonny ducked. But Rebecca slid her hand over Peter's bicep and held his arm down.

"Sorry, boys. No flour fights today," Rebecca said. "It's the maid's day off."

Jonny and Peter both sighed in disappointment. Then Peter dabbed a spot of flour onto Rebecca's nose. She laughed and backed away. "Just slice apples, okay, Tiger? The dough is almost ready."

Ruth-Ann didn't know what to think. She watched Peter and his new personality from a corner of the kitchen, feeling confused, searching for some secret in Peter's eyes. *What on earth is happening here?*

A week later, the mystery was solved.

Saturday night, Ruth-Ann, in a short blue-and-white pleated skirt and white silk top with a frilly lace collar and cuffs, paced the living room. She gripped a velvety blue cloche cap between her hands.

"Are you going out?" her father asked. He tapped the bowl of his pipe against his open palm.

"Yes. I expect so," Ruth-Ann answered, frowning, squeezing the cap. "Peter and I planned to go see some film shorts at the Vitogram, but he's late."

A few more taps of the pipe. He raised the stem to his mouth and made sucking sounds. "What are you going to see?"

"Oh, those people Peter likes. Fatty Arbuckle and Mabel Normand. He laughs till he gets hiccups."

Mr. Fear pulled the gold watch from his waist and read the dial. "It isn't like Peter to be late."

Ruth-Ann rolled her eyes. "It's strange. I haven't seen him all week. I feel as if he's *avoiding* me."

"Probably busy at the Victrola store."

"Maybe." Ruth-Ann sighed and gazed at the grandfather clock in the corner. "Something must be wrong. He's nearly half an hour behind." She scowled at her father. "We have to get one of those telephones, Dad. Everyone is getting them."

Mr. Fear had a cloth pouch raised over his pipe and was carefully emptying tobacco into the bowl. "You know my feelings—"

Ruth-Ann groaned, pumping her fists at her sides. "You think *everything* is a fad. Telephones . . . the Victrola. Dad, you said that *automobiles* were a fad!"

Her father laughed. "You know that isn't true, Ruth-Ann. I have come a long way in my thinking. When I was a boy, no one had electricity. That's the honest truth. And—"

"*Oh, poor you. Please* don't start that again. We all know how you had to light candles to read your homework at night and how the iceman brought big blocks of ice to keep the refrigerator cold."

She squeezed the cap in her hands. "If we had a telephone, Dad, I could call Peter and see why he isn't here."

Mr. Fear tamped the tobacco down with his thumb. "If I had a rocket ship, I could fly to the moon."

"You're not funny!" Ruth-Ann snapped, louder than she had intended. "I'm sorry—" She started to apologize, but the front doorbell chimed. "Oh. There he is."

Mr. Fear nodded and strolled out of the room, still fiddling with his pipe. Ruth-Ann ran to the front door, nearly tripping over the thick pile of the carpet.

She flung the door open. "Where have you been?"

Ruth-Ann gasped when she saw that it wasn't Peter. She stared openmouthed at Rebecca's friend Lily. "Oh. Lily. Hi. I—I thought you were someone else."

A sudden gust of wind fluttered Lily's long skirt. She grabbed her hat with one hand to keep it from blowing away. Ruth-Ann felt a few cold raindrops in the air.

"Lily, come in." She stepped back, and Lily slipped into the entryway. "Rebecca isn't here."

"I—I know," Lily stammered. "Ruth-Ann, I thought maybe you could do a favor for her. Is your father's automobile at home?"

Ruth-Ann squinted at her. "Well . . . yes."

"Your sister left this at my house." Lily held up a

small, silvery purse. The tiny rhinestones that covered the purse gleamed in the bright light of the entryway chandelier. "Can you take it to her? I'm late for a family party at my cousin's house."

Lily shoved the little oval-shaped purse into Ruth-Ann's hand. Ruth-Ann gazed at it. "Uh . . . where?"

"Rebecca is dancing at the Hot Bunny Club," Lily said. "She really needs her purse. I'm so sorry to bother you, Ruth-Ann. But can you drive over there and drop it off? She'll kill me if she doesn't get it."

"Well. Sure," Ruth-Ann said. "That isn't a problem. It's very nice of you, Lily." *My Saturday night isn't working out anyway*, she thought bitterly.

Ruth-Ann stood at the doorway and watched Lily run down the gravel driveway to her car. The wind swirled the shrubs in the yard, and raindrops pattered the front stoop.

"When Peter finally shows up, tell him to wait for me," she told her father. He was finally puffing on his pipe, in his favorite armchair in the den, with a book of Sherlock Holmes stories on his lap.

Ruth-Ann pulled on a rain slicker with a hood, grabbed the little purse, and made her way to the car, a 1922 black Pierce-Arrow coupe, at the top of the driveway.

The drive to the Hot Bunny Club was only about twenty minutes. But Ruth-Ann drove slowly, leaning over the steering wheel, peering through the curtain of raindrops on the windshield. The single windshield wiper was slow, and the wind kept making the car veer from side to side.

Questions slid through Ruth-Ann's mind. . . . *Where is Peter? Why is he so late? Why was Rebecca at Lily's? Is that where Nelson picked her up to go dancing?*

Gripping the wheel in both hands, staring hard into the white light of her headlights, she had to concentrate on driving.

She followed Bank Street to Division Street. Luckily, there were few cars on the road until she got to the Old Village. Her mum said the mayor had promised street-lights for all the major roads in town. But so far, there was no sign of them.

Traffic nearly slowed to a stop. With its small clubs and restaurants, the Old Village was always crowded on a Saturday night. Ruth-Ann wondered if Peter was at her house this moment, waiting for her.

The pink neon sign proclaiming THE HOT BUNNY CLUB, with red flames darting over a giant dancing rabbit, came into view just past the village. Ruth-Ann turned the car into the crowded lot. The tires crunched over the gravel surface. She slid into a parking spot under the neon sign.

She grabbed Rebecca's little rhinestone bag and stepped down from the running board of the car. The pink-and-red neon of the sign above sent a wash of color over her, and she suddenly felt as if she was inside the darting flames.

She began crunching over the gravel toward the low square building. The rain had stopped, but the wind still carried a chill.

A painted sign over the double doors of the entrance proclaimed: JAZZ DANCING GOOD FOOD NO ALCOHOL. Red flames were painted across the doors.

Ruth-Ann pushed the doors open and stepped into a pulsing room of shadowy bodies dancing in a swirl of purple lights. Blinking, struggling to adjust her eyes to the new light, she saw tables at one side, a long bar, a jazz band in tuxedos filling a small bandstand, and couples dancing. The music was deafening, a trumpet wailing high above the rest of the band, but voices and laughter somehow blared through the din.

A young man with oily slicked-back hair and a pencil-thin mustache, dressed in a checkered suit, moved quickly to greet Ruth-Ann. "I'm so sorry," he said. "We don't allow unaccompanied women. You must have an escort."

"I—I'm not staying," Ruth-Ann stammered. "I just need to give this to my sister." She raised the purse to the man's face.

He nodded and waved her toward the dance floor. Then he turned and headed toward the food tables.

Still blinking, Ruth-Ann took a few steps toward the center of the room. The band finished one number and began the next, a slow romantic waltz.

Ruth-Ann peered into the swirling violet lights, studying the dancers' faces. There were many couples swaying slowly to the soft song. But it didn't take long to locate Rebecca.

The purple lights made her blond hair glow. She was moving slowly, in a tight embrace. Her cheek was pressed against her date's face, and Ruth-Ann saw that she had one hand tenderly cupped at the back of his neck, gently stroking his skin and hair as they moved to the music.

And when they turned, Ruth-Ann sucked in a mouthful of air, felt the purse drop out of her hand, felt her heartbeat stop, felt her heart leap into her mouth.

Her legs started to fold. She stared. Stared at Peter in

Rebecca's arms. Peter's cheek pressed so tightly against Rebecca's. Rebecca moving with him through the haze of purple light, moving as if they had danced so many times before, moving as if they were one.

SIX

Of course, the little rhinestone clutch purse didn't belong to Rebecca. It was only Lily's way to get Ruth-Ann to the club. Lily wasn't Ruth-Ann's friend, but she was a decent person, and she must have thought that Ruth-Ann should know what was going on. That Ruth-Ann should confront the truth.

As she stared at Peter and Rebecca dancing, flames of anger, red as the flames on the neon sign, burned her chest. Her throat tightened. She had to force herself to breathe.

Ruth-Ann's first impulse was to hurtle across the dance floor, claw their faces, rip them both to shreds. But the driving pain in her chest and the haze of the lights and the dizzying shock held her back.

She kicked the rhinestone purse across the floor. Spun away, started to the door, bumping through couples just arriving. The picture of Rebecca's hand on the back of Peter's neck lingered in her eyes. And the dreamy expression on his face, eyes shut, lips turned up in a smile, refused to fade from her mind.

She crashed out of the club, shoving the double doors so hard, a couple screamed and stumbled back. And then she lowered her head against the rain, which had started up again, and ran over the gravel, into the pink-and-red neon reflection, to the safety of her car.

Panting like a dog, she sat behind the wheel, watching the raindrops slide down the windshield like sparkling red and blue jewels. How long did she sit there? She lost track of time. What did it matter? Peter wasn't back at her house waiting for her. Peter—her Peter—was wrapped in her sister's arms, pressed against Rebecca as if they belonged together.

"You don't belong together," Ruth-Ann said out loud. "Peter is MINE." Her breath fogged the windshield.

He isn't mine. He's Rebecca's, she thought. *He was all that I had, and now she has taken him, too.*

Ruth-Ann knew that the coppery taste at the back of her throat was hatred. She lowered the car window, leaned her head out, and spit—surprised to see the dark blood that spurted from her mouth.

Hatred.

Ruth-Ann didn't sleep that night. She paced her room, anger burning her whole body, her skin tingling, first icy, then hot, feeling the blood pulsing at her temples, pulsing until she couldn't think straight, couldn't form the words she wanted to say to her sister.

She heard Rebecca come home a little after midnight. She heard her sister in the hall, making her way to her room. Ruth-Ann froze in the center of her room, froze like a statue, and listened.

She knew she wasn't ready to confront Rebecca. She wanted to be in total control. *Ice not fire*, she thought. *Ice not fire.* But would her burning hatred allow her to speak to her sister without leaping on her and clawing her to death?

Peter was mine. I worked so hard to get him. I had to use so much magic, cast so many frightening spells to make him mine.

Now Rebecca waltzes off with him.

She thinks she's entitled to everything.

The next morning, Rebecca had already left for her job when Ruth-Ann came downstairs for breakfast. Like every morning, Rebecca had ridden downtown with their father.

Ruth-Ann spent the day in her room, trying not to cry, then giving in to it, hating herself for crying, hating Rebecca for making her cry, trying to stop . . . to think of something else. But, of course, that was impossible.

Peter isn't worth it, she told herself at one point.

But she knew that Peter wasn't the important idea here. Peter was just the *object* that Rebecca had stolen from her. Rebecca cared so little about her, loved her so little, that she would steal the only thing Ruth-Ann cared about.

Ruth-Ann tore at her hair. She beat her fist against her pillow. But she didn't explode until dinnertime, when Rebecca came into the dining room, hand in hand with Peter.

SEVEN

Ruth-Ann and her parents were just sitting down to a dinner of roast chicken and mashed potatoes, the aroma making Ruth-Ann hungry, despite the gnawing ache in her stomach.

Rebecca burst in, tugging Peter beside her. Her blue eyes flashed excitedly, and she had a tense grin that she could not rein in.

Ruth-Ann gasped loudly.

Peter glanced at her once, and his cheeks burned red. He lowered his eyes to the floor and didn't look her way again.

He was dressed more formally than usual, in a dark suit with a single-breasted jacket, a white shirt with a stiff collar that rose up to his chin, and a dark blue neck-tie, the knot tight against the collar.

"I have an announcement to make," Rebecca said in a trembling voice. She squeezed Peter's hand tightly. He kept his eyes on the floor. His whole face was red, as if his necktie was choking him.

"I know this family doesn't like surprises," Rebecca continued. She, too, avoided Ruth-Ann's eyes. Her eyes darted across the table, from their mother to their father, as if Ruth-Ann was not in the room.

"You hate surprises, but I hope this is one that you will accept with happiness," Rebecca said. She squeezed Peter's hand again.

Mr. Fear set down his fork. He narrowed his eyes at Rebecca, his expression tense. Their mother lowered her hands to her lap. Ruth-Ann saw that she was biting her bottom lip.

They are hiding their surprise at seeing Peter with Rebecca, Ruth-Ann thought. *But they both look about to burst. They do hate surprises; they hate anything that disrupts normal family life.*

"I might as well just spit it out," Rebecca said. "Peter and I are going to be married."

Ruth-Ann saw her parents' mouths drop open. Her

father made a choking sound. Her mother scooted her chair back noisily, as if about to stand up.

But Ruth-Ann was already on her feet. "No, you're not!" she shrieked. "No, you're not! No, you're not!"

Her hand sent the crystal water pitcher crashing to the table as she bolted toward them, screaming. "No, you're not! No, you're not!"

She slammed into Rebecca, who uttered a startled cry. Ruth-Ann grabbed her sister by the shoulders and shook her, shook her so hard that Rebecca made a gagging sound, and her arms flew up helplessly, and she sank to her knees with Ruth-Ann still gripping her shoulders and shaking her like a stuffed doll.

"No, you're not! No, you're not!"

The fury that Ruth-Ann had held in now roared out of her. Rebecca was on her knees, shrieking, crying for help, beating her fists weakly against Ruth-Ann's arms. Ruth-Ann slid her hands from Rebecca's shoulders to her throat and began to strangle her.

And that's when Ruth-Ann felt strong hands on her shoulders. Her father pulled her back. Peter wrapped an arm around her waist and tugged her off Rebecca.

Ruth-Ann pulled free of their grasp and stumbled back to the side table, sending two serving dishes and a flower vase shattering to the floor. Peter pulled Rebecca to her feet.

Sobbing, Rebecca rubbed her throat with both hands. Her long hair fell over her face in wild tangles. Her chest heaved in and out as she struggled to catch her breath.

Mr. Fear stepped between the two sisters, his arms outstretched to form a shield. "No more! Stop!" he cried. He turned his angry gaze at Ruth-Ann. "Control yourself. This is a civilized household."

"Ha!" Ruth-Ann cried bitterly. "What Rebecca has done isn't civilized." She glared at her sister, resisting the urge to attack her again.

"We—we couldn't help it." Peter spoke up for the first time. He had his eyes on Mr. Fear, not Ruth-Ann. "We—uh . . ."

"We fell in love," Rebecca said, her voice breaking. "It happened so quickly. But we know we love each other, and we want to get married."

Mrs. Fear cleared her throat. She stood gripping the back of her dining room chair, her face even more pale than usual. "This is something we all need to discuss, Rebecca. You can't burst in here at dinnertime and drop such big news on us, and expect that we can digest it immediately."

"I—I don't expect you to *digest* it," Rebecca snapped. "And we don't need to discuss it. It's my life and I'll do what I want to do."

Mr. Fear sighed. "You always have. We've always given you everything you wanted. But—"

Ruth-Ann let out a cry. "She just wants Peter because he was the only thing I had. No one else can have anything. She has to have it all."

"That's not true," Peter chimed in. He took a few steps toward Ruth-Ann, looking at her for the first time. Behind his glasses, his eyes were wide. His cheeks were still bright pink.

"We can't help how we feel, Ruth-Ann," he said. "We can't control our emotions. They control us."

"Very deep," she said sarcastically. "Did you get that line out of one of your magazines?"

"You wouldn't understand," Rebecca cried.

"I understand perfectly," Ruth-Ann shot back, crossing her arms tightly in front of her. She hugged herself, trying to force her heartbeat to slow.

"You think everything is about you," Rebecca said. "Well, this isn't about you. This is about Peter and me."

Peter nodded in agreement.

"I'm sorry you got hurt," Rebecca offered. But she

said it without any kindness or warmth. She took Peter's arm. "But you'll get over it. You're only seventeen."

"Get OVER it?" Ruth-Ann cried. "Get OVER it?"

Mr. Fear stepped between them again. "I think we need to take some time," he said. "Perhaps we could meet later tonight. After dinner. Or—"

Ruth-Ann let out a disgusted groan. "Are you really going to sit down and eat your roast chicken while she ruins my life?"

Mr. Fear waved both hands, signaling for Ruth-Ann to calm down. "This is difficult. This is a surprise," he said. "A surprise for all of us, and—"

She could see his mind whirring. She knew her father well. She could see when he was stumped, when he had no idea what to say next.

He's useless, Ruth-Ann thought. *He'll give in to Rebecca and do whatever she wants. He always does.*

And look at Mum. Standing there biting her lip, holding on to the back of the chair for dear life. She's useless, too.

"I'll tell you one thing right now," Ruth-Ann said. The words blurted out of her mouth before she had time to think about them. "You will *never* marry Peter. I'll make sure of that."

Rebecca tossed her head back and uttered a scornful laugh. "What are you going to do, Ruth-Ann? Cast a spell on us like some kind of witch?"

Ruth-Ann stared at her. "What a crazy idea."

EIGHT

After their dinner-table battle, the two sisters didn't speak. Ruth-Ann spent most of her time in her room. She also sneaked into her private attic, where she lost herself in the ancient books, delving into the spells and dark magic her family had practiced for nearly three hundred years.

She didn't have a plan. She imagined all kinds of revenge in her mind. She plotted against Rebecca, keeping her mind open about which course of action she might take.

She knew only one thing for certain: *Rebecca will never be married to Peter Goodman.*

Both of her parents pleaded with her:

"She is your sister. You cannot cut her off forever."

"You will get over your hurt. You will meet someone else. You are only seventeen."

"Peter isn't the man we would have chosen for Rebecca. But they are in love. You need to soften your heart, Ruth-Ann. Soften your heart and accept what will be."

Soften her heart?

Were they living some kind of fairy tale?

Prince Charming has chosen his bride, and now the kingdom shall rejoice! Hardly.

Ruth-Ann's heart only hardened at her parents' words. "Of course they have taken her side," she told herself. "Of course Rebecca can do no wrong. And I'm the one who has to accept it."

She spent hours sitting on the floor in the attic room in the middle of the circle of black candles. She read again about the horrifying curse between her family and the family named Goode. The history of bizarre murders and unimaginable evil.

Of course, the rivalry with the Goode family was all in the past. But it reminded Ruth-Ann that she was a Fear, that in these old books, she had the power of evil that her ancestors used.

Sometimes the whole idea made her laugh. Bitter laughter.

This is 1924. We have cars and telephones and electric lights. We are all modern today. There is no place for this old sorcery.

The old stories seemed impossible. Crazy. Like something out of the dime adventure novels that boys liked to read.

Still, the old books comforted her.

I have powers no one knows I possess.

One afternoon, Ruth-Ann was passing the library when she heard a familiar voice. The door was open a few inches. She stepped behind it to peer inside. She clapped her hand to her mouth, surprised to see her father talking with Nelson Swift.

Nelson, the forgotten man.

Nelson had made the big mistake of going away. Mr. Fear had sent him on a two-week business trip to the West. Two weeks that changed everything for Nelson.

Big, blond, brawny Nelson had been Randolph Fear's preferred candidate to marry Rebecca. And now the two men stood so tense, facing each other over the mahogany desk in the center of the room.

"I went to California for you. I settled your business

there because promises were made to me, Mr. Fear," Nelson was saying.

Ruth-Ann saw her father's face darken, his mouth form a scowl. He fiddled with his necktie. "You have to understand—" he started. "I . . . made no such promises. I—"

But Nelson interrupted. "Have you conveniently forgotten? I was led to believe I would become a part of this family."

Randolph Fear shook his head. "I'm sure I don't understand the minds of young women any more than you do."

"Have you no control over your own daughter?" Nelson slammed a fist on the desktop. "You are her father. Surely, she must obey you."

A humorless laugh escaped Randolph Fear. "Obey? Where do you live, Mr. Swift? In the nineteenth century?"

Nelson reacted with a growl. "My father is an attorney-at-law, sir. He has told me I could have an alienation of affections lawsuit against your daughter."

Ruth-Ann pressed her hand over her mouth to keep from making a sound. Nelson was threatening her father! She could see that Nelson was trembling, big drops of sweat rolling down his broad forehead. Did he know who he was trying to intimidate?

Mr. Fear remained silent for a long moment, fingering his necktie, his eyes locked on Nelson's. "Please take this news to your father," he said finally. "Tell him you may have *another* lawsuit because you have been dismissed from your job."

Nelson made a choking sound. "I—what?"

"You are fired," Mr. Fear said softly, barely above a whisper. "Please clean out your office by the end of the day."

Another long silence. Nelson mopped the sweat off his forehead with the palm of one hand. Ruth-Ann could see that he had sweated through the stiff collar of his shirt.

Nelson flashed Mr. Fear a final angry look. Then he spun on his heel and stomped to the door.

Ruth-Ann didn't have time to back away before he came storming out, shoving the door in her face. She cried out and stumbled back.

His eyes bulged in surprise when he saw her. "You haven't seen the last of me," he said, snarling the words. "I have ways of teaching your family a lesson."

"Get in line," Ruth-Ann said.

NINE

The wedding took place on a cliff top at Randolph Fear's mountain retreat in Colorado. A dirt road led up to the majestic lodge, built like a pioneer cabin, perhaps the biggest log cabin ever built. The building was wide and low, tucked into the rock outcropping behind it, chimneys lining the red slate roofs.

The mesa stretched beyond the lodge, tall grass and wildflowers on both sides of a winding path. Blue sky as far as you could see. The mesa ended in a jagged rock cliff, a steep drop to the canyon below with its dark boulders and a narrow ribbon of a river.

Beautiful—as if a painter had created a perfect rustic mountain scene. This was where Rebecca wanted her wedding. She said she wanted to be married at the top of the world, and this spot came close.

Ruth-Ann's parents begged her to come to the wedding rehearsal. But she refused, claiming she had a stomachache.

She had no intention of being part of the wedding party. She didn't plan to walk down the long white aisle with her mother and father. She planned to sit quietly near the back of the seating area, watch the ceremony, then retreat to her room.

The morning of the wedding, while everyone was having breakfast, Ruth-Ann sneaked out of the lodge and climbed the mesa to inspect the wedding site. The sky above her was cloudless; a red morning sun hung low on the horizon. A warm breeze hinted of the perfect day to come.

Ruth-Ann shielded her eyes with one hand and watched two red hawks swoop low overhead, then glide away.

Rebecca got her perfect day and her perfect setting for her perfect wedding.

An altar had been constructed at the top of the mesa. An arch had been built over that, and covered in white peonies and stephanotis. A narrow podium for the minister stood beneath the flowers.

The white-carpeted aisle stretched between two sections of folding chairs. The carpet made its way down the path to the lodge, tall grass and wildflowers swaying on both sides.

Ruth-Ann stood under the arch. The flowers smelled sweet. She gazed down over the edge of the mesa. Then she raised her eyes to the white flowers covering the arch.

This is where Rebecca will stand. This is where she will stand with Peter.

She suddenly realized she was making it all even more painful for herself. Why was she standing there? Why had she come up here this morning?

Abruptly, she turned and hurried down the aisle, following the carpet down the sloping hill to the lodge. She had a light breakfast. Then guests began to arrive.

The wedding was large. Her parents had invited two hundred people. But Randolph Fear would spare no expense for his eldest daughter. He had rented an entire train to bring them all to Colorado from the East.

After breakfast, Ruth-Ann retreated to her room. Lily was the maid of honor. Of course, Ruth-Ann hadn't been asked.

Her parents had bought her a dress nonetheless,

violet with white lace, long pleated skirt to her ankles, a cute vest over a frilly top. She didn't want to dress up. Still, Ruth-Ann had no choice but to wear it.

The wedding was scheduled for one o'clock. As Ruth-Ann got dressed, she heard scurrying in the hallway, excited voices. Last-minute preparations had everyone tense.

A knock on her door startled her. And when she pulled open the door, she had an even bigger surprise.

Rebecca stood there. She was in her wedding dress but held the sparkly tiara-shaped headband in her hand. The dress was a beautiful ivory, open at the back, beaded all over, with lacy butterfly sleeves and a filmy sweep train flowing down the back. Her hair was tied with a wide silk ribbon so that it flowed like a golden waterfall down the back of the train.

"Ruth-Ann—" she started. Then she stopped and narrowed her eyes, as if she didn't know what to say next.

Ruth-Ann pulled the door open a little wider. "Rebecca? What are you doing here?" She couldn't hide the coldness in her voice.

"I—I need you to forgive me," Rebecca stammered. "Please, Ruth-Ann. I know what I've done. I know I've hurt you. But . . ."

Ruth-Ann had never seen her sister so unsure, so nervous, almost unable to speak. She took a step back, allowing Rebecca to enter the room.

Rebecca rolled the sparkly white headband between her hands. "Please say you forgive me," she said, locking her blue eyes on Ruth-Ann. "Please say it. I'll spend the rest of my life trying to make it up to you. I promise."

Ruth-Ann's mouth dropped open. Was Rebecca really saying these things?

"It's my wedding day," Rebecca said. "I need for it to be perfect. And it won't be perfect unless I have my whole family behind me, especially you."

The two sisters stared at each other. The silence grew heavy and awkward. Finally, Ruth-Ann relented. "Okay," she said in a whisper. "I forgive you."

"Oh, thank goodness!" Rebecca cried. She flung her arms around Ruth-Ann. She pressed her cheek against Ruth-Ann's. Her cheek was hot and wet with tears.

Ruth-Ann pushed her back gently. "You're going to spoil your makeup."

Rebecca stepped back, wiping her eyes. "Help me with this headband, okay? And with the train. It got all twisted."

"I forgive you, but I won't walk down the aisle,"

Ruth-Ann said. "I'll be there for you, Rebecca. I forgive you. I really do."

"That's enough," Rebecca said, taking both of Ruth-Ann's hands in hers. "Thank you, Ruth-Ann. Thank you."

They were the last words Rebecca ever said to her sister.

TEN

The white flowers on the arch ruffled in a light breeze. The sun floated directly above the mesa, hovering in a robin's-egg-blue sky.

Ruth-Ann took a deep breath. The air up here smelled so cool and sweet. She sat in the fourth row of seats, to the left of the aisle, pulling her silk violet hat over her hair, arranging her long skirt, the ground soft beneath her shoes.

A buzz of voices surrounded her. Peter's family had already taken their seats at the front on the other side of the aisle. Ruth-Ann admired the dresses worn by a group of cousins edging their way into the row in front of her. Everyone in their most colorful finery. The men in such dark, serious suits and the women in their fanciest plumage, colorful as birds.

She craned her neck to survey the guests behind her. A solitary figure caught her eye. She shielded her eyes from the sunlight and squinted.

Nelson Swift?

Yes. Nelson in a pinstripe suit, a black necktie pinching his starched white collar. Nelson, his light hair blowing in the wind, his face locked in a blank stare at the altar.

Why was Nelson here? Why did he travel all the way to Colorado? Ruth-Ann knew for a fact that he hadn't been invited. His name hadn't been mentioned in her house since the day he threatened Randolph Fear and lost his job.

Ruth-Ann had an impulse to go back to his row, to walk up to him and just demand, "Nelson, what are you doing here?" But she was settled in her seat, and she would have to disturb four or five others to get to the aisle.

Instead of getting up, she stared hard at him, hoping her mind waves would draw his attention. But Nelson kept his gaze on the altar, his expression blank, mysteriously vacant.

Ruth-Ann heard oohs and aahs. She turned, thinking the wedding ceremony had started. But the guests were reacting to a large red hawk that soared low over the mesa, floating with raised wings, then vanishing below them.

The voices all stilled as the organist, a young man in a black tuxedo, began to play. *How did they get an organ up here?* Ruth-Ann wondered. They must have brought it in a horse cart.

Ruth-Ann raised her face to the sun. The warmth felt soothing, almost calming. She settled back in the chair, thinking about how happy she was not to be in the wedding party.

I can enjoy the spectacle, she thought.

But when Peter appeared, doing his slow walk up the aisle between his two parents, she suddenly felt cold, as if the sunlight had disappeared.

Will all my old feelings come rushing back to me?

Will my anger, my feelings of betrayal, my dismay at being cheated of the boy I cared about—will they all come sweeping in now and send me back into dark despair?

Ruth-Ann held her breath and watched Peter walk up the aisle with his parents, watched and waited for the powerful feelings to return.

No. She was fine. A single shudder shook her body. She was fine.

I can make it through this. I'm going to be okay.

Peter's mother wore a satiny blue dress, the skirt short, the back cut out, and had a bell-shaped cloche hat pulled down over her straight gray hair.

That outfit is much too young for her, Ruth-Ann thought. *Does she think she's the bride?*

Ruth-Ann was amused by how much Peter resembled his father. They both had owlish round faces and wore circular, black-framed eyeglasses.

Peter had his dark hair parted in the middle and so slicked down with hair oil, his head reflected the sunlight. He wore a stephanotis corsage on his lapel and had a bright purple handkerchief in the pocket of his suit jacket.

Not his usual style, Ruth-Ann sneered. *He looks so nervous. Why doesn't he at least force a smile?*

Jonny Penderman followed. He was Peter's best man. In contrast to the groom, Jonny had a wide, goofy grin on his face, as if he thought the whole thing was a hoot.

Ruth-Ann's parents walked arm in arm toward the altar. Her mother already had tears in her eyes. She dabbed at her face with a white lace handkerchief. Randolph Fear winked at Ruth-Ann as they passed.

Lily followed them, looking lovely in her simple cream-colored maid of honor dress, a satiny sash tied in a graceful bow at her waist. Ruth-Ann watched the five bridesmaids march in and form a line facing the altar.

Then all eyes turned to the back as the bride approached the altar. Beautiful Rebecca. A tense smile frozen on her face. A bouquet gripped tightly between her hands. Her normally pale face slightly flushed from her excitement. Her eyes on Peter as she walked slowly, gracefully along the white carpet.

The parents took their seats. The minister appeared behind the podium. Ruth-Ann squirmed, trying to see him better. But the bride and groom blocked her view. She saw that he was tall and thin and tanned with a shock of white hair over his forehead. "Welcome, everyone!" he exclaimed. "Welcome. Welcome, everyone."

He had to shout. Ruth-Ann knew that her father had wanted to try one of those newfangled loudspeakers he had read about. He had contacted the Edison Company to see if they had one that would work. But he was disappointed to learn that no loudspeaker could work since there was no electricity on the mesa.

"We are gathered here today to join Rebecca Ellen Fear and Peter Arthur Goodman in holy matrimony."

The minister lowered his eyes to the podium as he began the ceremony.

His voice drifted in and out of Ruth-Ann's hearing. A burst of wind brought his words loud and clear. When the wind reversed, he sounded muffled and far away.

Peter and Rebecca held hands as the minister spoke.

The sight of them there. The perfect wedding tableau. Everyone so good-looking and well dressed and happy. The lucky couple with their hands clasped, already united even before the ceremony was over.

How could Ruth-Ann *not* feel bitter?

She gritted her teeth, her whole body suddenly tense. She tried to slow her pounding heartbeats. She shifted in her seat, the minister's words flowing past her, not really hearing them, only hearing a steady drone of voice and wind.

And then she heard the words clearly as the minister gestured to Peter, raising both hands. "And now . . . you may kiss the bride."

Ruth-Ann saw people arching forward, twisting in their seats, to get a better view. The big, happy conclusion. The kiss that everyone anticipated.

Peter turned to Rebecca. He didn't smile. Squinting, Ruth-Ann was surprised to see a blank, emotionless look on his face.

And then people gasped as he bent and lifted Rebecca off her feet. He picked her up and held her in front of him.

And whispered voices rang out all around Ruth-Ann . . .

"How romantic."

"Look. He picked her up to kiss her."

"So adorable. The most romantic thing I ever saw."

Holding Rebecca like a baby, Peter lowered his face to hers and kissed her lips. And as they kissed, he walked to the edge of the mesa. He held the kiss for another few seconds. Then he raised her in his arms and tossed her over the side of the cliff.

Rebecca's shrill scream would linger in everyone's ears for weeks, even though it lasted for only a few seconds.

ELEVEN

Time froze for Ruth-Ann. The world stopped.

Rebecca's scream faded as she plunged to the ravine below. She fell too far for anyone to hear the crunch of her landing, but Ruth-Ann imagined it.

A shudder shook Ruth-Ann's body. And in that brief moment of frozen horror, what lingered in her mind was the expression on Peter's face as he carried her to the cliff edge. The empty eyes, the blank stare. As if he was no longer inside himself, as if he had *vacated his own body*.

Screams rang out all around her. Guests leaped to their feet, faces pale, mouths open. But no one moved. There was nowhere to go. Nowhere to escape or erase the horror of what they had just seen.

Children wailed. Screams and screeches of horror and disbelief rang off the mesa walls.

Ruth-Ann's eyes refused to focus. The people around her became a colorful blur. Loud sobs and shouts and animal moans rose, more and more shrill, until Ruth-Ann clamped her hands over her ears. It was then she realized she was screaming, too.

And then she saw a dark blur rise up in front of her. Someone lurched forward and grabbed her by the shoulders. Grabbed her and shook her.

He finally came into focus. Her father. His face red, radiating anger. His eyes bulging. He kept shaking his head, his lips moving but making no sound.

He dug his fingers into the shoulders of her dress and uttered a curse through gritted teeth. "YOU did this!" he screeched, spit flying into Ruth-Ann's face. "You killed your own sister!"

"N-no—!" Ruth-Ann stammered. She tried to pull free of his painful grasp. "No, Father—"

"You did it! You did it!" he screamed, shaking her. Her hat flew off and landed in the grass at her feet. "You swore she would never marry Peter, and you kept your promise!"

"No!" Ruth-Ann screamed. "No! How could I?

You've got to believe me, Father. I didn't. I didn't!"

Some guests were running down the hill to the lodge. Others stood sobbing, shaking, comforting one another. A small crowd circled Ruth-Ann and her father, watching their angry confrontation.

Randolph Fear uttered a string of curses. He shook Ruth-Ann hard. "You put a spell on that boy. I know you did. Think I didn't know what you were doing up in that attic room? Did you really think you could cast a *spell* and I wouldn't know?"

"No, Father!" Ruth-Ann cried. "No!" And then a frightening thought flashed into her mind. "You—you know about that room. *You* know those spells, too—don't you, Father?"

His grip on her arms tightened. His dark eyes burned into hers.

"It was *you*!" Ruth-Ann screamed. "*You* did it. You—you *monster*! You killed your own daughter!"

"You are *insane*!" her father growled.

"NO!" The cry burst from Ruth-Ann's throat. She pulled back with all her strength—and broke free. Broke free of her father's two-handed grasp.

She stumbled backward, the pain of his grip still on her shoulders. She thrashed her arms, bent forward, struggling to catch her balance.

But she couldn't stop. The thrust of her attempt to free herself sent her hurtling backward. Nothing to grab on to. Nothing to stop her.

And she went tumbling over the side of the cliff. Her hands grabbed the hard dirt on the cliff edge, then slid away. And Ruth-Ann fell, without a scream, without another breath. Fell straight down in a flurry of cold wind, the blue sky stretching wide above her. Joined her sister after a moment of crunching pain . . . and then darkness.

TWELVE

Randolph Fear dropped to his knees on the grass. He held his head in both hands. He covered his face and didn't move. Only his shoulders shivered, revealing that he was sobbing.

The circle around him tightened. No one spoke. The screams had died. The only sounds were the sobs and muffled crying of those who remained on the mesa top.

When Randolph raised his head, he looked for his wife. He saw two women walking with her, holding her arms, helping her to the lodge.

Randolph didn't bother to wipe away the tears that stained his reddened cheeks. "What did I do?" he said to those standing around him. "What did I do to deserve this?"

His shoulders shook again, and a sound escaped his throat, a choking sound. "I . . . lost two daughters. Two daughters on a day that was supposed to be full of joy. Why? I did nothing. I am innocent."

A man reached out to help Randolph to his feet. But Randolph shoved his hands away. He gazed around. "Where is Peter Goodman? Where is he? He married my daughter, then threw her away. Where *is* he?"

"He isn't here," a woman called. Her face was tearstained, too. She dabbed at it with a damp lace handkerchief. "I didn't see him leave."

Randolph uttered a loud sob that ended in a hiccup. "Peter murdered my daughter. Then he vanished? Can this be happening? Do nightmares really exist in the daytime?"

A shadow fell over Randolph. Still on his knees, he shivered. He raised his eyes to the young man in a dark suit who stood above him. In his grief, it took his mind a few seconds to recognize the man.

"Nelson Swift."

Nelson nodded solemnly. He held his hat tightly in one hand.

"Mr. Swift." Randolph squinted up at him. The sun over Nelson's head cast his face in shadow. "Why are you here?" Randolph's voice came out in a quavering whisper.

Nelson hesitated. "I . . . came to tell you . . . But . . . I was too late."

"Tell me? Tell me *what*?" Randolph Fear demanded.

"It's about Peter," Nelson replied. "I learned the truth about him."

"Truth? Spit it out, Mr. Swift. Tell me what truth."

"His name isn't Peter Goodman," Nelson said. "His name is Peter Goode."

Randolph gasped and covered his face again. "The curse . . . ," he murmured. "The curse between our families . . . the Goodes and the Fears . . . It continues."

Huddled there on the grass, he realized the truth . . . all of it. Peter wasn't under a spell. Randolph had accused his daughter Ruth-Ann unjustly. No one had cast a spell on Peter to force him to murder Rebecca.

Peter was a Goode. Because of the curse, a Goode and a Fear could never marry. He murdered Rebecca of his own will. Murdered her for revenge against the Fears.

But revenge for *what*?

Randolph raised his hands and let Nelson help pull him to his feet. "It won't end today," Randolph murmured. He leaned heavily on Nelson as they began to walk to the lodge. "Now I will have to take my revenge on the Goodes. It won't end. Not before I have avenged my daughters."

Nelson guided him between the tall grass on either side of the carpeted aisle. He didn't speak. He didn't know what he could say.

Nelson heard again in his ears the screams of the two girls.

Maybe it will never end, he thought.

A burst of wind carried the girls' dying screams back to his mind. He shut his eyes and guided Randolph Fear down the mesa to the lodge.

PART TWO

THIS YEAR

THIRTEEN

I laughed and ran my hand through Max's silky blond hair. "Max, Robby and I can't be *identical* twins," I said. "Because he's a boy and I'm a girl."

His serious blue eyes were locked on mine. I could see he was thinking hard about it. My cousin Max is only five, but sometimes I think his brain is much older. He always seems to be thinking hard about things.

"Harmony, are you and Marissa twins?" he asked finally.

I had to laugh again. "No. We're just sisters."

"But you look a lot like her," he said. His eyes went to the driveway of the lodge, where Dad was helping Marissa unload all her bags and suitcases from the van.

Robby should have been helping them. He promised he would. But Robby has a way of disappearing whenever there's any heavy lifting.

"Marissa is five years older than me," I said.

Max grinned. "I'm five." He held up the fingers on one hand.

"But we're sisters so we look alike," I said. "Same black hair, right? Same blue eyes? Same string-bean bodies?"

He shrugged. He was losing interest. Five-year-olds didn't have great attention spans, I knew, unless they were craving candy or ice cream. I babysit Max a lot, and whenever he thinks sweets are a possibility, he develops a one-track mind.

I shielded my eyes from the sun, which was floating high over the red tile roof of the lodge. A shadow soared low over the long log-cabin-styled building. A bird with a wide wingspread. Maybe a hawk.

"Max, look where we are!" I exclaimed. I took his hands and swung him around to face the mesa. "We're on top of a mountain in Colorado. Do you believe it?"

He got that thoughtful look on his face again. "Can we go skiing, Harmony?"

My mouth dropped open. "Huh? It's summer. You

can't ski in the summer, silly." I squeezed the shoulders of his red T-shirt. "Besides, we're here for a wedding, remember? Marissa is marrying Doug tomorrow."

He scrunched up his face. "You have to get married on a mountain?"

The kid is hilarious. But I had to be careful. Sometimes when I laugh at him too much, he gets hurt, and his angry pout is epic.

"Is this the first wedding you've ever been to?" I asked.

He nodded.

"Well . . . people like to get married in beautiful places. And our family used to own this place, and we came here every year when Marissa and I were little girls. And Marissa always thought it was the most beautiful placc on carth."

In front of the lodge, Dad had Marissa's wedding gown in its layers of plastic wrapping draped over his shoulder. He was struggling not to let it touch the driveway. Marissa followed him, carrying her big makeup bag.

Robby suddenly appeared and came jogging over to them. "Can I help? What can I carry?"

Dad rolled his eyes. "It's all done. You're too late."

"Where *were* you?" Marissa demanded.

Robby shrugged. "I had to do a thing—"

"Oh, shut up," Marissa snapped. "We know where you were. On the phone with Nikki."

Our brother, Robby, is obsessed with Nikki Parker, and Mom and Dad can't stand her. That's why she wasn't invited to the wedding, which totally pissed Robby off, of course. He's been bitter and horrible and about as obnoxious as he can be about it, which is a lot.

He and I are seventeen, but guess who is the grown-up? And it's not just that girls are smarter than boys, which everyone in the world knows. I mean, it's proven by science.

Robby has always been shy and gotten nowhere with girls. I mean, we're both seniors this year, and Nikki is his first real girlfriend . . . ever. Can you imagine?

Now maybe I'm not one to judge. I like boys. Mom and Dad think maybe too much. But I don't see what's wrong with enjoying yourself and having fun when you're a teenager. Especially if you're careful.

What I'm saying is, Nikki is cute, but she's just as immature as Robby. And my parents hate the way she's always nuzzling his neck and tickling him and being very physical in front of everyone.

Robby loves all that, but my parents aren't physical people. Dad kisses Mom on the cheek sometimes. Of course they love each other, but they just don't always show it.

Dad says they're private people, and that's fine with me. Because they keep their privacy, and I keep mine. I hardly share anything with them. Why would I? They more than likely wouldn't approve, and there's no reason to look for trouble.

I try to like Nikki but it's hard. She's kind of . . . flaky. You know. Sometimes I overhear Robby helping her with her homework, and I don't want to say she's dumb. But she's not . . . deep.

Again, I shouldn't talk. I got into Penn by the skin of my teeth. (Nikki's going to the junior college in Martinsville, the next town, because her parents can't afford to take out a big student loan.)

And Robby? He says he needs a gap year. You know. To find himself. He says maybe he'll travel or something. But I know the truth. If he stays in Shadyside, he'll be able to see Nikki all the time. I told you, he's obsessed.

Mom and Dad are furious about it. They think Robby should get out of the house and start his life like everyone else. They blame Nikki and say she's a bad influence on

Robby. I'm sure that was one reason Nikki wasn't invited to Marissa's wedding. Just meanness on their part.

There's no reason to sugarcoat it. My parents can be mean when they want to. After all, we are Fears, and the Fear family has a long line of incredibly mean people. There's even a book about us, about our family history and how messed up we are.

A black SUV pulled up the gravel driveway to the lodge entrance and pulled in next to our van. Doug Falkner, the groom, and his buddy Harry Marx, the best man, piled out and stretched their arms and backs as if they'd driven two thousand miles or something.

I watched them gaze at the lodge and then turn to see the mesa, the tall grass sloping up, away from the building, up to the sharp rock cliff. Harry said something and they both burst out laughing. Harry is the comedian in the group.

I don't think Doug has much of a sense of humor. I've never heard him make a joke or anything. I mean, he's okay, I guess, but he's serious a lot of the time. He has a stare that's kind of intimidating. It reminds me of a bull with his head lowered, staring at the matador, trying to decide whether or not to attack.

I don't know where that came from. But Doug *is* kind

of a bull. He's big and wide and bulked up, and he talks in this low growl . . .

Okay. I admit it. I don't think he's right for Marissa.

But no one ever asked me. And remember? I keep my mouth shut.

So I called out to Doug and Harry and, waving, went running across the grass to them. They waved back. But I stopped halfway with a thought. "Where's Max?" I asked it out loud.

I shielded my eyes and made a complete circle, searching for him. I was supposed to be watching him while Uncle Kenny checked in at the front desk. Where did he disappear to?

"Max? Hey—Max?"

Then I spotted him. My heart stopped beating and a scream burst from my throat. "Noooo!"

He stood at the edge of the mesa, looking down at the rock cliffs at his feet. He leaned over the side, as if daring himself, or maybe trying to get a better view.

And I screamed again. "Max—get back! Get away from there! Max—step back!"

That's when his knees bent, his arms flew up, and he started to tumble over the side.

FOURTEEN

With a desperate leap, I hurtled behind him and flew into the air. I wrapped my arms around his waist and pulled him from the cliff edge.

My heart was pounding so hard my chest hurt, and I struggled to catch my breath. I held on to Max, my arms tightly around him, until he ducked and squirmed away.

He tossed back his head and uttered an insane giggle. "Harmony, did you really think I was going to fall?"

I stared at him, my mouth open, still unable to breathe. "You mean . . . you did that on purpose?"

He giggled some more, and nodded with a grin plastered on his face.

"You devil!" I cried. I grabbed him with both hands and shook him as hard as I could. It only made him laugh harder.

Then, so pleased with his little joke, Max took off without another word, running on his spindly legs down the path to the lodge. And I saw his dad, my uncle Kenny, standing at the entrance, watching us.

Did Kenny see the close call on the cliff edge? If he did, I'd hear about it. Uncle Kenny looks like a lemon with his round face and his shaved head. And he acts sour as a lemon, too.

Make a list of my least favorite family members, and look—there's Kenny at number one. He's bitter about his divorce, even though he got full custody of Max. He's bitter because he's an assistant manager at some kind of cardboard box factory, not even an actual manager.

He has a total thing about my dad. Kenny is Dad's older brother, but Dad has had all the success with his real estate properties all over the state. Dad has made a lot of money. We have a pretty nice house in North Hills, the fancy part of Shadyside, while Kenny and Max live in an apartment in the Old Village.

But so what?

Is that a reason to be a total obnoxious jerk?

And wouldn't you know it—Kenny gave the first toast at the rehearsal dinner that night.

The whole wedding party was at one long table in the dining room. The lodge is very rustic. The pinewood walls and the low, log rafters across the ceiling give it a real pioneer look.

Pink and white lilacs were everywhere. That's Marissa's favorite flower. And everything about the wedding is pink and white.

Marissa sat in the center, across the table from me, and she looked beautiful. She had her hair down, falling past her shoulders, the top held back loosely with sparkly rose-gold bobby pins. She wore a pale pink sweater over faded jeans. It wasn't a dress-up kind of event.

Doug sat next to her, and she kept squeezing his hand. He should have been smiling, right? I mean, it's a wedding dinner, you know? But he had his bull face on for some reason and didn't even look at Marissa that much.

I was on the other side, down at the far end of the table, next to Robby, and then Max, and then Uncle Kenny at the very end.

My parents were a mile down in the other direction.

But somehow I managed to hear their whispered conversation. And I'm pretty sure I heard Dad telling Mom, "What was wrong with that nice med student, Aiden? I wish Marissa was marrying him tomorrow."

Everyone was talking, and there was a lot of clatter of dishes and silverware. But I'm sure I heard Dad correctly. Mom's face turned red. She's the easiest blusher on the planet. I didn't hear her reply.

I knew they both preferred Aiden, with his plans to be an orthopedic surgeon. He was handsome and well dressed. I thought he was *too* pretty and *too* full of himself. But I haven't liked any of Marissa's boyfriends.

Anyway, it didn't matter. Aiden was gone.

The dinner was going pretty well. I mean, whenever the Fear family gets together, it isn't all sweetness and light, or peaches and cream, or whatever the expression is. We all have strong personalities and usually the personalities clash.

We were all here for a wedding, however, and for once, everyone was on their best behavior.

Well . . . except for Max. Maybe he was excited because it was a big party. But he kept waving his empty glass in the air and shouting, "Wine! I want wine! I want wine!"

Uncle Kenny thought it was hilarious. He didn't do anything to stop Max. And that encouraged my little cousin to keep his shouts up even longer.

It was a nice meal. A creamy Caesar salad, followed by lobster bisque, then chicken and mashed potatoes, and Brussels sprouts with chestnuts and bacon.

I kept watching Marissa and Doug. I was waiting for Doug to smile just once. But he ate with that same flat expression on his face and didn't talk much to Marissa or to my aunt Hannah, who sat on his other side.

Hannah spent her time talking to Grandpa Ernie Fear. Everyone calls him Grandpa Bud. I don't know why. Bud is my dad's father. He's got to be eighty-five or more, but he's as sharp and energetic as anyone. He's even on Facebook. He's an old white-haired rascal, and he has to be my favorite of everyone in the family.

When Uncle Kenny began tapping his glass with his fork and stood up to give a toast, my throat clenched up. I had this feeling of dread, mainly because Uncle Kenny always insists on giving the first toast at any party, and he usually embarrasses himself and the people he is toasting.

Well, he didn't fail me.

Kenny raised his nearly full glass of red wine. Max tugged his shirt. "Dad, what's for dessert?"

Kenny shoved his hand away. "Max, I'm giving a toast." Kenny cleared his throat for a long time. "Hello, everybody. Can you hear me?" he boomed. "I seem to be down at the far end of the table. Someone put me down here in Siberia. Guess I'm being punished for something, ha-ha."

No one reacted to that. We all know how Kenny likes to complain.

The ceiling light shone over Kenny's lemon head. He really did look like a talking lightbulb.

"I know the wedding is going to be done better than my chicken," Kenny continued. "It was a little pink inside. Doug and Marissa, I hope salmonella isn't one of your wedding gifts! Ha-ha-ha."

Kenny has a horrible, grating laugh. Kind of a choking sound. It sounds more like vomiting than laughing.

"But what's a little raw chicken on such a happy occasion?" I saw Mom down at the other end roll her eyes and groan. Marissa squeezed Doug's hand. Her expression was tense.

"I want to toast a beautiful bride," Kenny said, shoving his raised glass toward Marissa. "Of course, I've known Marissa since she was born and, believe me, she wasn't always this pretty. Face facts. You were an ugly baby, Marissa. You looked a lot like Yoda—you know—from the *Star Wars* movies, except maybe not as cute."

Kenny's grin grew wider. He thought he was being hilarious. Didn't he notice no one was laughing?

"And now look what you've turned out to be," he continued. "So beautiful and so graceful and artistic. I mean, really."

He lowered his glass. "Marissa, do you remember the first time you were onstage? What were you—first grade? Kindergarten, maybe. That Easter show at your school. And when you went out there, you were so scared, you peed on the stage? Remember? They had to stop the show and mop it up?"

A few people laughed uncomfortable laughter. Marissa tried to push a smile on her face, but she couldn't hide her embarrassment. Doug laughed and shook his head.

I could feel the tension around the table. I shut my eyes and prayed, *Please make him stop. Please let this be over.*

But Kenny droned on. "I'm just pushing your buttons, Marissa. It's all said with love, believe me. Of course, I've got some other good stories to share with Doug. But this isn't the time. I just want to say—unnnnnh—"

I still had my eyes closed, muttering to myself. But I

snapped alert when Uncle Kenny started to choke.

He coughed a bit, a hoarse cough. Then his eyes bulged and his face turned bright red, and he made horrible choking sounds. The wineglass fell out of his hand and crashed onto his dinner plate, and wine ran over the table.

I jumped to my feet and watched as Kenny, choking, reached into his mouth. His fingers fumbled inside his mouth. We all gasped when he pulled out a large gray feather.

It was like a pigeon feather, only maybe a little bigger. Kenny held it in front of him. His hand was shaking. He squinted at it in disbelief.

"The chicken really *was* undercooked!" Grandpa Bud joked.

Kenny thought the danger was over. But he started to gag again. He was wheezing and choking. He reached into his mouth, and another long feather slid out.

"Uh . . . I . . ." He tried to talk. But he started to choke again. The two feathers had fallen onto his wine-soaked dinner plate. And now he pulled a third one, an even longer feather, from his open mouth.

People jumped to their feet. Mom buried her head in her hands. Dad was hurrying toward our end of the table.

"We need a doctor," he shouted. "Someone call 911!"

Doug pulled out his phone and started to call. Marissa had turned her back. She hates anything ugly or scary.

Kenny slid another feather from his mouth. Then, his shoulders heaving, his face as purple as a plum, he pulled out two more.

"What is going on?"

"How is this happening?"

"Is it some kind of trick? Is this one of his awful jokes?"

"It's impossible. I'm sick. He's making me sick."

The roar of voices rang off the low rafters. Everyone was up from the table now. Max was standing on his chair, staring at his father and bawling his head off, big tears running down his cheeks.

"911 isn't answering!" Doug shouted over the confused, horrified voices. "It just keeps ringing."

Dad and I helped Kenny down to the floor. Kenny pulled out another handful of feathers. His hands were shaking and he was making horrible gagging sounds.

We rested him sitting up against the wall. He gazed up at us, kind of glassy-eyed, like he was in shock. There were long gray feathers everywhere. Piled on the table, scattered on the floor. Kenny groaned and made raw animal noises. He was breathing so hard, his chest heaved up and down.

And then the horrible throat sounds stopped. Kenny slumped forward, shut his eyes, and didn't move.

"Kenny? Kenny?" Dad grabbed him and shook him. "Kenny?"

Holding on to Kenny, Dad turned to me, his face wide with horror. "I think he's dead."

FIFTEEN

No one moved. A tense hush fell over the room. Mom had picked up Max and was comforting him. Grandpa Bud came up and stood beside me. He placed a hand on my shoulder.

"Kenny?" Dad's voice trembled.

Kenny made a noise like *glurrrrrp*, and he threw up all down the front of his shirt. I heard groans and sighs of relief around the room. It was disgusting, but at least Kenny was alive. And the feathers had finally stopped coming.

I grabbed a couple of dinner napkins off the table and handed them to my uncle to clean himself up. Kenny looked dazed. He kept blinking and shaking his head.

"Kenny, should we get a doctor?" Dad said. "Are you okay? Can you talk?"

Kenny rubbed his neck. "I have such a sore throat," he whispered.

"We'll get you to your room," Dad said, starting to pull him to his feet.

"Did that really happen?" Kenny whispered.

"See? Your dad is just fine," Mom said. She had brought Max over to see that all was returning to normal.

"Did Dad eat a *bird*?" Max demanded.

We all laughed, more from relief than anything else.

Max wasn't making a joke. The poor kid was just totally confused. And who wasn't? Who could explain what we just saw?

Around the room, people muttered and shook their heads. What we had just seen was *impossible*.

"This place is cursed," Dad whispered to me. He wasn't just upset. He was angry. "I begged your sister to have her wedding at home. This lodge is a cursed, terrible place. That's why the family sold it."

"Shhh." Grandpa Bud poked Dad in the side. "Shut up, David. We don't have to talk about it. Everyone knows what happened here."

"I don't know about it," I said, grabbing Bud's sleeve. "Tell me."

Before he could answer, a woman's voice rang out over all the confusion. "Sorry I'm late, people!" I turned. It was Rita Gonzalez, the wedding planner my parents had hired. Talk about bad timing. "Is everyone having a good time?" she chirped. "Are you all ready for the rehearsal?"

Well, we took half an hour to get ourselves together. Dad said Kenny was resting okay in his room. I went back to my room and decided to change. I had the smell of vomit on me. And I kept picturing those huge feathers Uncle Kenny kept pulling from his mouth.

Why was I chuckling?

I could hear my brother, Robby, through the wall. He was in the next room, and of course, he was on the phone with Nikki. I heard him telling her about Kenny and the feathers. She probably thought he was making it up.

They started having some kind of argument. They always argue about everything. I think that's conversation to them. Robby kept saying, "Deal with it. Deal with it." I clicked on the TV on the wall to drown them out.

The evening sky was a purple gray as we all made our way up the path to the mesa. A white altar stood near the cliff top, and it glowed in the light of a pale half-moon.

Grandpa Bud took my arm and I helped him walk up the sloping hill. "Have you seen Max?" I asked him. "Is he back in the room with his dad?"

"They put Max to bed," Bud said, squeezing my arm. His hand felt brittle and cold. "It was his bedtime, I guess. But also he was very upset about Kenny."

"Understandable," I said, watching Marissa and Doug step under the arch over the altar. Rita Gonzalez had her clipboard raised and was reading off something to the bride and groom, who I could see from all the way back here were only half paying attention. They were holding hands and gazing down at the canyon below.

Grandpa Bud squinted at me. "*You* were upset?"

"Of *course*." I could feel my face go hot. Why was he studying me like that?

He stopped walking but didn't loosen his grip on my arm. "Harmony, do you really not know what happened on this spot?"

I hesitated. "Well . . . I read about it a little bit."

He nodded but didn't reply. We started walking again.

"The groom and the best man will stand here," Ms. Gonzalez was saying. "They will lead the wedding march. The parents will follow and . . ." She gazed around. "Where's the best man?"

I saw Harry Marx stumble on the grass and struggle to stay on his feet. It was obvious that he'd had too much wine at the rehearsal dinner. Harry wore ragged shorts that came down almost to his knees and a T-shirt that read: *I'm just here for the food.*

His lips were moving. He was singing to himself. He stepped up to the edge of the cliff and began flapping his arms above his head, pretending to fall.

"Not funny, Harry!" Marissa shouted.

"You're acting like a five-year-old," I told him. "Max already tried that!"

"Come over here so we can get this over with," Doug said.

I saw Rita Gonzalez flinch. "Please be careful," she said. "I think we all want it to be perfect tomorrow."

"Sorry," Doug muttered. But he didn't smile or try to charm her or anything.

Tomorrow is their wedding day, I thought. *Why aren't they more into it?*

Harry stumbled his way up behind Doug. He grabbed Doug by the shoulders and tried to wrestle him to the ground.

Marissa shook her head. "Come on, guys. You really are acting like five-year-olds."

"No. Six-year-olds," Harry said. He rubbed the top of his head with a fist and made monkey sounds.

Ms. Gonzalez moved him a few steps to the right. "You'll walk up the aisle, taking slow steps to the music, and you'll land right here. Okay?"

Harry touched his forehead in a two-fingered salute.

Meanwhile, Doug had pulled Marissa away from the altar, and they seemed to be having some kind of argument. They were both talking at once, but quietly so they couldn't be overheard. Marissa kept shoving Doug's chest with an open hand.

Mom came up beside me, her eyes on the arguing couple.

"What's up with them?" I asked.

She brought her face close to mine and whispered, "Wedding jitters. Happens to everyone."

"Seriously? Shouldn't they be all over each other?"

Mom laughed. "Why don't you tell them that?"

"Parents? Where are the parents?" Ms. Gonzalez called, motioning with her clipboard.

Mom hurried away. Dad was helping Grandpa Bud into a chair.

I gazed around at the rest of the wedding party. Everyone was quiet, grim-faced, solemn. It didn't seem like a celebration.

I guessed that the bird feathers pouring out of Kenny's mouth had totally freaked out everyone.

Doug's parents were cute. They were older than my folks and looked more like grandparents than parents. They both had matching short white hair and round, jolly faces.

Chubby. Not obese, but you know. Their stomachs bounced a little when they walked. Their hands were doughy like cartoon hands and their fingers were kind of like sausages.

I'm not trying to be cruel. I liked them. They were sweet.

They were the only ones who dressed up for the rehearsal, so they definitely looked like they were from a different family.

The four parents gathered around Ms. Gonzalez, who began pointing to where they should go after walking up the aisle. I saw Robby at the back of the rows of folding chairs. He actually lowered his phone from his ear. Maybe Nikki had to take a bathroom break.

I walked over to him, my hands tucked in my jeans

pockets. "How's it going?"

He shrugged. "Okay, I guess. I keep clearing my throat, thinking I have a feather in there."

I laughed.

"I'm serious," he said. "It happened to Uncle Kenny. It could happen to anyone. My throat has been tickling ever since."

"I feel weird, too," I confessed.

"How do you mean?"

"My stomach is, like, heavy. I just have this feeling. Like something bad is going to happen."

"Harmony, something bad already happened," Robby said.

"No. I mean. Worse," I said. "You know what happened on this spot before, right? At another wedding that our family had here?"

"No. What happened? Someone died?"

"Well . . . yeah," I said, surprised that he didn't know the story. "Didn't you read that old book about our family?"

"I skimmed it."

"Huh?"

"It was too weird."

I stopped. Something caught my eye at the edge of the

107

tall grass beyond the chairs. "Robby, what's that animal? See him?" I pointed.

He squinted into the moonlight. "Is it a raccoon? No. A gopher, maybe?"

I took a few steps toward it. "I think it's just a squirrel. Look— it's standing up on its back legs."

The animal scampered forward and came into clear view in a shaft of moonlight. Then two more appeared behind it, moving out from the tall mesa grass. Their little round eyes flashed in the moonlight.

"Yes. It's just a squirrel," Robby said.

"Aren't they cute?" someone said.

"Look how they're standing up."

"Somebody take a picture."

But then I counted five more squirrels, darting out of the grass, running on all fours, then stopping in a ragged line and standing up, raising their small paws in front of them.

Ms. Gonzalez turned away from the group at the altar, and I saw her eyes go wide. "What are those doing here?" she cried. "Where did they come from?"

More came scurrying in front of the chairs. Grandpa Bud climbed to his feet as they scrambled a few inches from him.

And now there were more than a dozen squirrels, scurrying toward the altar, and somehow they didn't seem cute anymore. There were too many of them. It looked like the ground was moving.

They ran a few feet, then stopped. Stood up on their hind legs. Then ran some more.

Marissa let out a scream as two squirrels hurtled into her, bumping her ankles. She danced to get away. Doug grabbed on to her to keep her from falling, and squirrels swarmed between his legs.

Some women screamed. More squirrels came shooting out from the tall grass. They were running down the aisle between the chairs, swarming over the ground, scampering over shoes and bumping into people.

Doug's mother let out a cry and began thrashing her arms in the air as two squirrels ran up her legs.

"Look out!" someone screamed.

I stumbled back. Dozens more squirrels stampeded toward us.

Dad was slapping at his legs, trying to throw the animals off him. The air filled with screams and the thuds of animals bumping everyone.

Marissa held on to Doug. Doug was slapping and squirming, trying to shake a squirrel from his hair. He had another one on his back and one climbing one leg of his jeans.

"What is *happening*?" Ms. Gonzalez screamed. "It's on my face! It's on my *face*! Help me! *Somebody!*"

The screams echoed through the darkening night sky.

SIXTEEN

"I helped Grandpa Bud back to the lodge," Robby told me. "He wasn't hurt or anything, but he said his heart was beating like crazy. He said thank goodness he remembered his pills."

I tsk-tsked. "Did you see Dad trying to pull that squirrel from Mrs. Falkner's hair? She was hysterical. It wouldn't come off."

"One of Doug's friends sprained his ankle trying to get back here," Robby said. "I guess we're lucky more people weren't hurt."

We were in my room, still a little breathless after our escape from the squirrel stampede on the mesa. I sprawled on the plum-colored bedspread. Robby sat hunched in the armchair across from me. His hair was damp and matted to his forehead. He had scratches on one arm from an attacking squirrel.

"It was like a nightmare," he said.

"A true horror show," I said, puffing up the pillow behind my head. "You know, Dad told me this place is cursed. He said he begged Marissa to have her wedding at home."

Robby snickered. "Like Marissa would ever listen to him."

"Maybe she should have," I replied. "I mean, first Uncle Kenny is choking on feathers. Then—"

A hard knock on the door made me sit up. I glanced at Robby. "Who is that?"

"Only one way to find out," he said. He was tumbling his phone in his hand. I could see he was dying to call Nikki and tell her the latest.

I pulled open the door. Grandpa Bud stood there with his hand raised, about to knock again. I saw he had changed into baggy khakis and a red-and-black lumberjack shirt.

His cheeks were pink, and his eyes looked tired. He studied me for a few seconds and didn't smile. "Harmony, can I come in?"

"Of course," I said, pulling open the door and stepping back.

Behind me, Robby scampered to his feet. "Grandpa Bud, are you okay?"

Bud didn't answer. He shuffled across the room toward the armchair.

"Crazy out there," Robby said. "It's like . . . it couldn't happen, right?"

Grandpa Bud didn't sit down. He turned at the chair and pointed a finger at me. "I know what you did," he said softly.

I wasn't sure I'd heard him correctly. "Excuse me?"

"Don't play innocent, Harmony," he said, his voice stronger now. "I know what you did."

Robby put a hand on Bud's shoulder. "Want to sit down?"

Bud obliged. He perched on the edge of the chair and kept his eyes on me. I could feel my face going hot and I knew I was blushing.

"Harmony, do you think I don't know those spells?" he asked.

Robby shook his head. "Spells?"

"The feathers," Bud said. "The squirrel invasion. Harmony, I can do those in my sleep."

My heart was pounding now. My muscles all went tense. I leaned back against the pine dresser and crossed my arms in front of my chest.

"I can tell you which of the old books those spells come from," Bud said. "I've even *done* that feather gag myself."

My brother's face was twisted in total confusion. "You mean—?"

"Did you forget I'm a Fear? I'm eighty-six years old. I've had a lot of years to practice the family magic." He coughed, then muttered, "Some would call it sorcery. I believe that's what we are. Sorcerers. By line and by blood."

I opened my mouth to speak, but I didn't know what to say. I was caught. Bud nailed it. He was right about me.

He turned to Robby. "And you. Did you have anything to do with this? Are the two of you working together?"

Robby shrugged. "No way. I didn't even know—"

"Well, how is that possible, Robby? Where *were* you?" Bud snapped.

"He was probably on the phone with Nikki." I finally found my voice.

Bud rubbed his chin, his eyes locked on me. "I just have one question for you, Harmony. Are you only having fun? Or are you trying to ruin your sister's wedding?"

I swallowed. My heart was pounding like crazy. "Uh . . . a little of both," I finally choked out.

I hadn't counted on being caught. And the truth was, I didn't really know *why* I was causing the mischief. I mean, I have a lot of resentment against Marissa, I admit it. But I didn't want to totally ruin the wedding. I guess I just wanted to make it . . . more exciting?

All this endless wedding nonsense. . . . All the solemn talk and months of planning. . . . The food . . . the band . . . the minister . . . the rehearsal dinner . . . blah blah blah.

I just had to do *something*.

Grandpa Bud scooted back in the chair and rested his head against the chair back. "Harmony, you have to be careful here," he said, rubbing his hands on the arms of the chair. "It's possible for magic to get out of hand in this place. I mean out of control. Even the simplest spells—"

"I don't have anything else planned," I blurted out.

"Even the simplest spells can go in unpredictable directions," he continued. "This is a cursed place. There is an evil about it that has led to horror and death."

"I know," I started. "I read—"

But Grandpa Bud was determined to tell us the story.

"It was a wedding here much like this one. With two sisters. Their names were Ruth-Ann and Rebecca. They were Fears, and one of them—the bride—had made a terrible mistake. She had chosen for her groom a young man from the Goode family."

I settled onto the bed and folded my arms around a pillow held to my chest. Of course Robby and I knew about the Goode family. We knew the families have been enemies for hundreds of years. And we knew there was a curse that a Fear and a Goode could never get together—and live.

I tuned out as Bud continued with the details of the wedding. My mind kept jumping around. I wondered if he would snitch to my parents about what I had done. And, whoa. If Marissa ever found out, she'd never speak to me again.

"*Both* sisters died on that day," Bud was saying when I tuned back in. "It was in the early twenties, something like ninety-five years ago. Before I was born. But I grew up hearing my parents talk about it. They were there. They saw everything, all the horror, all the sadness. And that day gave them nightmares for the rest of their lives."

Robby had been listening intently. I don't think he knew any of this. Somehow he was never interested enough in our family.

"What happened to the Goodes?" he asked. "We haven't heard anything about them. I mean, Mom and Dad don't talk about them. And I never knew anyone named Goode."

"They haven't been heard from," Bud said. "Not since that awful day. Not since that day the bride and her sister died."

"So they're gone?" Robby said, twisting his phone in one hand. "Then maybe the curse between our families is over?"

I tossed the pillow aside. "You don't think there's a Goode here at *our* wedding, do you, Grandpa Bud? You don't think—"

He shook his head. "Believe me, your father did a very thorough background check on Doug and his family. He hired two different firms to investigate them. They're not Goodes. Not related to them in any way."

"What about Doug's family's guests? And his friends?" Robby asked.

Bud shook his head. "None of them are Goodes. You can be sure of that."

I sat up. "So then what's the problem, Grandpa? Okay, so I played a few tricks, had a little fun. Indulged my inner . . . sorceress. I know it was wrong. I know it was a little mean. But there's no real harm."

Grandpa Bud narrowed his eyes at me, and his expression turned grim. Suddenly, it appeared that all the color had drained from his face. He was as pale as the window curtains beside his chair.

"If you love your sister, Harmony, you'll stop this right now. History can repeat itself. Listen to me. I've seen it! History can repeat."

A cold shudder shook my body. Bud's words rang in my ears. And as he spoke, I had this terrifying picture in my mind. I saw Marissa sailing over the cliff edge, hanging in the air, her arms flailing, her hair flying above her head, her mouth open in a silent scream. And I saw her fall straight down, straight down for miles, straight down—to the rocks below.

SEVENTEEN

My hands were still shaking and my body felt cold as I helped Grandpa Bud to his feet, and he lumbered out of the room without another word.

Robby shook his head. "I mean, wow. What a weird night."

"Yeah, weird," I muttered. I was struggling to force that frightening picture from my mind.

"I can't believe you did spells and, like, didn't tell me," Robby said.

"Why spoil the surprise?" I replied.

He stared at me. He has no sense of humor. "Harmony, teach me."

"What?"

"Come on! Teach me how to do things like that!"

I frowned at him. "Why? What for?"

"Well . . . maybe I could cast a spell on Mom and Dad to make them like Nikki."

"That would need to be a *very* powerful spell," I said.

"No. Seriously—"

"Get out of here," I said, opening the door. "I'm not teaching you any magic tonight, and I'm sure you're dying to call Nikki and tell her about the squirrels."

He stopped at the door. "Should I tell her *you* caused the squirrel stampede?"

"Don't you dare!" I shouted. "I'll kill you if you tell anyone, Robby. I'm serious." I waved my hands like I was casting a spell. "I'll turn you into a frog. No. I'll turn you into a *wart* on a frog. Do you get what I'm saying?"

He laughed. "My sister the witch."

"Sorceress!" I called after him. Then he disappeared down the hall to his room.

I stood at the door, my hand gripping the knob, taking deep breaths, trying to feel calmer. I couldn't decide what to do next. I had an impulse to go to the hotel bar and see if any of the cute guys Doug had invited were there.

I always read about people who hook up at weddings.

I mean, it would take my mind off being caught by Grandpa Bud, and the worry that my little dabbling in magic might get out.

But frozen there at the door, staring out into the glare of the long hallway, I suddenly felt terrible. A wave of guilt washed over me, so powerful I felt weak at the knees.

I'm not a good person like Marissa, I'll admit it. Marissa would never think about going to the bar to find someone to hook up with on the night before *my* wedding. She's a total straight arrow, and it works for her.

Maybe Marissa was the answer. I should go see her. Not to confess. Forget that. But to be a good, supportive sister on the night before her wedding.

I only meant to be a little naughty, not to ruin her weekend entirely. We've never been the closest, but I knew I'd feel better if I talked to her and showed her I was here for her.

I clicked the room door behind me and started down the hall. I could hear Robby on the phone in the next room. I prayed he wasn't snitching on me, telling Nikki that I was behind all the bizarre happenings.

Two girls I didn't recognize passed me. They were about my age, around seventeen. One was blond; the other had red hair in a cute bob. They must have been Doug's guests. One carried an ice bucket, the other a couple of bottled Cokes. We said hi but we didn't stop.

I knocked on Marissa's door. "Marissa! Are you in there?"

I heard some shuffling sounds. Then footsteps padding across the room. Marissa pulled open the door and couldn't hide her surprise that it was me. "Oh. Hello."

She had changed into a loose silky nightgown that came down past her knees. She was barefoot. Her dark hair was pulled back off her shoulders into a messy topknot. I saw immediately that her eyes were red-rimmed. Had she been crying?

"Are you okay?" I said.

"No." She stepped back so I could enter the room. I gazed around. It was as neat as if no one was staying in it. All of her clothes were stowed away in the closet and drawers, I imagined. Her wedding dress was draped over the armchair.

We both dropped onto the edge of the bed. For a moment I couldn't take my eyes off her light blue toenails. Marissa never bothered with things like nail polish. But now she was all decorated, blue fingers, blue toes. (It's her favorite color. Her eyes are blue, too. So pale blue that sometimes they're gray.)

"What's wrong?" I asked.

She scrunched up her face. "Everything."

I took her hand. It was kind of awkward. I mean, we never hold each other's hands. "Tell me. What's so terrible?"

She sighed. "Well . . . where should I start?" Then it all spilled out of her in one breathless burst. "Doug is being a beast, and I don't know why. Uncle Kenny says he's going to sue the chef because of all the feathers. Two of Doug's cousins sprained their ankles, tripping over squirrels on the lawn. Aunt Dora may have broken her hip. They took her to the hospital in town. Didn't you hear the ambulance?

"The woman who is supposed to do my hair and makeup tomorrow just called and said she's too sick to come. I just checked the weather online and it says rain for tomorrow."

She was gasping now, her chest heaving up and down.

"Take a breath," I said. I squeezed her hand, then she pulled hers away.

"I'm not going to cry. I don't want a puffy face at my wedding. But I really wish I could. So far, this wedding is a *disaster*. I can't decide if it's a comedy or a tragedy."

"Choose comedy," I said. "Listen, Marissa, it's going to be beautiful. The weather way up here is always different from what they say. I'll bet it'll be bright sunshine."

She shrugged. "I don't know . . ."

"Do you honestly think *yours* is the first wedding where things are tense?" I was trying to be sweet and understanding, but somehow that didn't come out the way I wanted. Why did I have so much trouble being sympathetic to her?

"So some crazy things happened," I continued. "But just think . . . the sun will rise, and tomorrow will be a totally different day. Everything will be different. You'll be *married*! Can you believe it?"

She didn't smile. Her eyes locked on mine. "I know you don't like Doug," she said.

"Yes, I do—" I started.

"I know you don't," Marissa said softly. "But he'll be a good husband. He's steady and reliable. He'll take good care of me."

What a weird, old-fashioned thing to say.

"I like Doug," I said. It sounded awkward, at least to me. "Everyone likes Doug."

She just gazed back at me, her face a blank now.

I knew that Doug wasn't the love of Marissa's life. Everyone knew it. Aiden Murray was the love of her life. She met him in college, and she adored him.

When she brought Aiden home to meet our family, Marissa was so excited she could barely speak. It was obvious to all of us that he was crazy about her, too.

And then I ruined it for them.

I didn't mean to. I really didn't. But I did ruin everything for them, and I know it's the reason why Marissa and I will never be close.

EIGHTEEN

I stayed in her room a while longer, and Marissa and I chatted about less serious things. We talked about Max and what an impossible little troublemaker he is. We talked about her dress, and she showed me two different pairs of shoes. She couldn't decide which was best. They were both perfect, of course.

We talked about Robby and how obsessed he was with Nikki. Marissa said she begged our parents to invite Nikki, but they said the wedding was already too big for the lodge.

Marissa rolled her eyes. "Of course, it had *nothing* to do with how they think Nikki is all wrong for Robby," she said sarcastically.

"They think she's a psycho," I said, chuckling. "They're not wrong. I mean, some of the things she says are just nuts. She has no filter at all."

Marissa nodded. "And Robby loves it. He thinks she's a rebel. She's so *out there* all the time. She doesn't even try to control herself."

We were silent for a moment.

"And what's with Doug?" I asked casually, trying to keep it light.

She shrugged again. "No clue. I thought he'd want to spend some time with me tonight. But instead, he went off with some of his friends."

She pursed her lips. "I don't get it. He already had his big bachelor party in Atlantic City, which he won't tell me anything about. Why did he choose to hang with the guys again tonight?"

"He's probably just nervous," I said, scrambling for an answer. "Just needed to blow off some steam. Doug lets things build up, right? He isn't really good at talking about stuff."

She nodded. "Yeah. I guess you could say he's bottled up sometimes." She stared at the wall, as if she'd never thought of this before.

"Well, after tomorrow, you can put the handcuffs on,

chain him to the living room couch."

She smiled but she didn't laugh.

I couldn't tell if I was cheering her up or not. But I knew *I* was starting to feel a lot better. "Know what we need?" I said, jumping to my feet. "We need a few beers. Follow me to the bar?"

She thought about it, then shook her head. "I don't think so." She swept her hand back through her hair. "I need my beauty rest, you know?"

She stood up and followed me to the door. I turned and we hugged. It was a genuine hug, an honest moment between us. Maybe we could start to be closer. Well . . . that's what I thought.

I decided to take a walk. Breathe some fresh air. I walked through the lobby. I could hear music and voices from the bar down the hall, but I kept walking to the front doors.

I found myself in a cool, windless night. A blanket of clouds above blocked out the moon, and I couldn't see any stars. Uh-oh. Maybe it *was* going to rain tomorrow.

A wide paved path led around the front of the lodge, and I followed it to the other end, walking behind a low evergreen hedge lined with spring flowers, mostly azaleas and crocuses and freesias, and a few daffodils.

I took deep breaths. It smelled sweet. Heavenly. I had this flash: I could lose myself in the night. Everything felt so fresh and alive.

The path led down, away from the lodge. Someone had planted a long row of apple trees, and their blossoms were mostly on the ground, already fallen, light and white as feathers.

I turned back. The darkness was rich and black. The light escaping from the lodge windows didn't reach this far down the slope.

What would happen if I just kept walking?

I guess weddings give you all kinds of crazy thoughts.

I kept thinking about Marissa married. Marissa and Doug. Just as they had planned in high school.

High school sweethearts. Marissa and Doug.

His family couldn't afford to send him to college. He went part-time to the community college in Martinsville, and he worked at his cousin's furniture store.

Marissa went off to Wisconsin to go to school in Madison. But they promised they'd stay together. They wouldn't fall apart. They promised each other to stay true.

Sweet story, huh?

The memories swirled in my head. The combination

of the faces, the names, the memories, and the heavy sweet fragrance of the flowers and the air—it was all making me feel high. Kind of light and giggly. You know, that floating feeling, where everything is a blur and you don't mind it at all?

I stretched and raised my face to the sky. If only I knew a spell to keep this moment alive forever. . . .

A shiver ran down my back. I was suddenly chilled. I turned and started to climb up the path. Light from the lodge windows rolled over me, and I began to feel heavy again, back down to earth.

The front driveway came into view, and then the lodge entrance. And I stopped with a gasp and watched a tall figure step out of a red sports car and go loping toward the entrance.

Was that . . . *Aiden*?

No. It couldn't be. I was still lost in the whirlwind of memories. Aiden Murray wouldn't be here. No way.

But he was as tall as Aiden, and broad-shouldered. He had that athletic, forceful stride, and he wore that same stupid newsboy cap over his curly blond hair, the hat that everyone teased him about.

He stopped and talked to a tall, red-haired valet. He gestured toward the red sports car, and the valet handed him a ticket. Then, adjusting his hat, he turned and stepped into the light of the lodge entrance.

And I saw his face.

And started to run toward him, my shoes slipping on the dew-wet path. "Aiden? Is that you?" I shouted. "Aiden?"

NINETEEN

"Aiden?"

He disappeared into the building. The front doors whooshed shut behind him.

I took off running, my shoes scraping the dirt path. I was nearly to the entrance when the red-haired valet stepped in my way. "Nice night," he said. The name on his uniform badge read: *Walter Q.* "You taking a walk?"

I nodded. "Yeah. The path. Very nice." I tried to edge past him.

"There's an even nicer path around the other side," he said. "Lots of wildflowers. Of course, you can't see them at night."

"I . . . have to catch up to my friend," I said.

He nodded. "Okay. Have a good one."

I pushed open the doors and stepped into the lobby. No sign of Aiden anywhere.

It was late. There was no one behind the front desk. I could hear voices and music from the bar. I trotted down the hall to check it out and look for him there.

My eyes must have been playing tricks on me. There was no reason for Aiden to come to Marissa's wedding. Not after what happened. I knew for sure that no one had invited him.

The little purple-and-gray bar off the hall was crowded. I recognized most everyone. They were from the wedding party. Doug sat at the end of the bar with a bunch of his buddies clustered around. They were clinking beers and laughing a lot.

Marta, Uncle Kenny's ex-wife, sat at a low table across from my aunt Dawn. They both stared at martini glasses in their hands.

No sign of Aiden.

My cousin Sarah waved to me from a stool against the back wall, but I pretended I didn't see her. The memories about Aiden were washing back to me, like ocean waves on a beach, one after another, an endless sweep of memories.

I gave the bar one last search. Then I hurried to my room. I wanted to be away from the laughing voices and the clinking glasses and the faces. . . . Away from all those faces, so I could remember.

I kicked off my sneakers and settled back on the bed, rested my head against the soft, padded headboard, and let the memories come, let the waves wash over me, cold and steady, chilling as they were, chilling and painful in so many ways. . . .

A year ago. No. A little more than a year ago. It was April of last year. Spring break and we were all looking forward to seeing Marissa, hearing about her semester, her adventures in Madison.

She always came back from college bursting with stories and funny anecdotes. She loved it at Wisconsin. I pictured her fluttering her arms like a bird—so happy to be free, so happy to be away from Shadyside and starting a real life on her own.

She was nice to me on those visits. I don't really think she missed me when she was there with all her friends and her classes and the orchestra she played in. We'd talk maybe every two or three weeks on FaceTime. But our conversations were always short and awkward, and I could never think of anything interesting to say.

I was going through a serious guy phase. I was kind of crazed. I was hanging out with three—or four? I can't remember exactly—different guys that year. So there was *no way* I could talk to Marissa about that. But when she came home during vacation breaks in her chirpy, excited, enthusiastic mood, she was nice to me, and even caring.

But believe me, we were all shocked when she came prancing into the house, pulling Aiden behind her. "This is Aiden," she announced, as if that was explanation enough.

Mom and Dad acted as if they weren't the least bit surprised, but, of course, they had to be. Robby and I tried to act cool, too. But I was stammering and maybe blushing a little, and couldn't stop staring at him.

I mean, she could have warned us, right? It's not like our family is big on surprises. Like, Dad gave Mom a surprise birthday party on her fortieth birthday, but he made sure he told her about it in advance. Get the picture?

And, of course, Doug was the 800-pound gorilla *not* in the room. I knew we were all thinking about Doug and how Marissa had vowed to wait for him as we stared at Aiden and tried to be casual.

You might expect Aiden to be a little uncomfortable, meeting us all for the first time, seeing that we had absolutely no warning from Marissa that she was bring-ing him. But he seemed totally calm, almost relaxed.

He had that little newsboy cap pulled over his curly blond hair, and he had a bit of reddish-blond scruff on his chin. He wore a black bomber jacket that looked per-fectly broken in over faded jeans torn at both knees.

His eyes kind of sparkled. I know it sounds dumb but they did. They were big and dark. He had a warm, toothy smile, a soft voice, and he had this adorable little dimple in his chin.

I thought he was hot. I confess, it was like an instant attraction. I had this strong, ridiculous urge to kiss him just to see what it would be like.

Staring at him and trying not to look like I was study-ing him from across the room, I wondered what it was like when you were close to him. I wondered what he smelled like.

That's totally weird, isn't it?

And it's not like I'm usually jealous of Marissa. I mean, I don't have a sick thing about wanting everything she wants or trying desperately to be like her. But I had this feeling about Aiden. Love at first sight, maybe? Ha.

Marissa held his hand and told us how they'd met at a fraternity party that neither one of them had been invited to. They both crashed the party, and it gave them something to talk about when they bumped into each other. "We already had something in common!" Aiden exclaimed.

Robby laughed too hard at the story. Mom and Dad just nodded with these strange smiles frozen on their faces. I knew they were studying Aiden intensely, and they probably thought he was some kind of hipster with that hat and the beard and the tattoo creeping up his arm where his sleeves were pushed up.

Yes, I'm sure they thought he was some kind of arts major. Maybe a musician, not like good old solid Doug, who was already working in a furniture store and taking business courses—trying to make something of himself.

And then we were sitting around in the living room, drinking white wine to celebrate Marissa's return for spring break (a special treat for Robby and me since we were still sixteen) and enjoying Mom's great blondies. That was when Aiden revealed that he was premed and planned to be an orthopedic surgeon.

After that, my parents loosened up. Maybe that was the moment they decided to forget about Doug, too. I don't know.

I remember that I kept thinking about Doug and

wondering if Marissa had told him. And *if* she had told him, *how*?

Did she break up with him over the phone? Send a text message that said, "It's over"? Marissa couldn't be that cruel. I knew that for sure. But she certainly wasn't mentioning Doug now. Maybe Aiden didn't know about him.

So everyone was settling in, having a nice conversation. Aiden was talking about his parents in Milwaukee. They were both doctors, and that's why Aiden was inspired to become one, too.

Robby was playing *Candy Crush* on his phone while we talked. He can never do one thing at a time. He always has to do at least two or three. Marissa asked me about my woodworking classes. I was actually flattered that she remembered.

"I'm really into it," I said. I didn't tell her that I took the class because a really hot guy named Zack was taking it, and I wanted to get to know him. Funny thing was, I quickly discovered I seriously liked working with wood—and I had a knack for it.

Zack and I hung out a few times, but we weren't really into each other. He was too quiet and sincere for me. But I kept showing up at the woodworking class because I wanted to get really good at it.

"I'm building a cabinet in the basement," I told Marissa. "I'll show it to you later."

Aiden squinted at me like I was weird or something.

"My dad has a workshop in the basement," he said, setting down his wineglass. "Actually, it's more like a studio. He does bronze busts of people. Very big heads." He laughed. "He isn't any good at it. He admits it himself. His heads are all lopsided. But it helps take his mind off his work."

"How lopsided are they?" I asked.

"Well, they keep rolling over onto their sides," Aiden said. "They don't stand up."

We were laughing about that when Nikki came in. She burst into the room, crept up behind Robby, and mussed up his hair with both hands.

"Hey—!" he cried out angrily, but then he saw who it was, and he laughed.

Nikki is all arms and legs, and she was wearing a seriously short skirt, black and straight, and so tiny I thought it might be a belt. But she likes to show off those long legs.

She looks like a garden fairy with her white-blond hair in that undercut pixie, that pointy chin, and those enormous green eyes.

"Nikki, come meet Aiden," Marissa said.

"Okay." Nikki grinned and plopped down in Aiden's lap. "Hi," she said. Then she tugged hard on a lock of his hair until he cried out.

"Nikki," I said. "Why'd you do that?"

"Because he's cute," she said. "You're cute, aren't you, Aiden?" She tugged his hair again, more gently this time. Then she climbed out of his lap, laughing.

"Um, nice to meet you," Aiden said. He turned to Marissa. "Is she always like this?"

Marissa rolled her eyes and nodded.

"I have that same hat," Nikki said, removing the hat from Aiden's head and examining it. "Yep. I thought so. It's a girl's hat."

"Nikki—" Robby started.

"But it looks good on you," Nikki said. She handed it back to Aiden. "Are you and Marissa a thing?"

"Yes. We're a thing," Marissa said.

"Well, he's adorable," Nikki said.

"Glad you approve," Marissa replied.

I could see that Nikki didn't get Marissa's sarcasm. She sat on the arm of Robby's chair and mussed up his hair again.

The conversation turned to the Shadyside High

Tigers. The basketball team went to the state finals, but lost in the first round. Then Marissa had some stories about her friends in Wisconsin.

And that's how it went. Pretty comfortable, actually, considering there was a surprise boyfriend in the room. Everyone agreed Mom's blondies were the best. Dad talked about how long our family had lived in Shadyside. "We were here almost since the town began. They even named a street after us."

The seven of us were having a nice, relaxed get-to-know-Aiden chat.

A pleasant evening.

And then, two nights later, I did something crazy.

TWENTY

I've had a long time to think about it, and I still can't really explain why I did it. I'd like to blame it on the wine. I'd had two big glasses that night, and I'm not used to wine.

Robby and I drink beer at our friends' houses all the time. But we never have wine. And I could really feel it. I mean, my head felt kind of feathery and the room was tilting a little bit.

But that doesn't really explain all of it.

In the couple of weeks before Marissa came home with Aiden, I'd gone kind of crazy. I'd skipped school a few days to hang out with some older guys by the river. Just for the danger of it, I guess. Just for a little excitement.

Yeah. Excitement. Maybe what I did that night was because I wanted excitement. I mean, is there anything more boring than eleventh grade? When you're not even old enough to drive?

Well, okay. Maybe I'm just making excuses. And there is no excuse for what I did.

The memory is still so fresh in my mind. And it comes up to haunt me no matter how I try to force it away, to push it back.

I read in a science magazine that brain scientists now know how to go into your brain and remove certain memories. Seriously. They can find the place where a memory lives in your brain and remove the cells that hold it.

If you have a sad memory that you want to lose, they can find it and remove it.

Creepy?

I don't read a lot of science magazines, but that story seriously freaked me out. And if I could have someone go into my brain and pull out the memory of what I did that night last April, I would say, *Do it*. I wouldn't hesitate for a second.

I guess it started when Marissa was mean to me. It was a Saturday morning, and I slept in. When I shuffled down to breakfast, still in my nightshirt, still yawning, Marissa was waiting for me.

It wasn't exactly an ambush, but I was only half awake, and it felt like an ambush to me. She slid the orange juice carton across the table, her expression thoughtful, like she was going over what she planned to say to me.

"Harmony, I'm having a bunch of my friends come over tonight," she started.

I didn't really want orange juice. I reached for the box of Frosted Mini-Wheats. "Nice," I murmured. "From high school?"

She nodded. "Yeah. You know. Taylor and Olivia and Dani. They're all in town. A few others from the orchestra. To meet Aiden."

I nodded. "Cool." I reached for the sugar. I know it's crazy to put sugar on Frosted Mini-Wheats, but that's the kind of person I am.

"I don't mean to be harsh," Marissa said slowly.

Uh-oh, I thought. *She's about to be harsh.*

"But it's my old friends and I really want them to have a chance to know Aiden and . . ." She hesitated. Her eyes locked on mine. "Maybe you could make plans of your own tonight?"

I took a breath. "You mean—"

Her cheeks flushed pink. She turned her gaze away.

"Well, you've been hanging out with us constantly since I got home. Which is fine, of course. But . . . I'm a little worried that you don't have friends of your own. I mean—"

"Don't worry," I snapped. "I have plenty of friends. I have a life, Marissa."

"Well, you've been sticking so close to Aiden and me." Her voice trembled. She had to know she was being cold. "Like . . . like moss on a tree."

That made me laugh. "Me? *I'm* moss on a tree? Are you kidding me?"

"Just saying." Marissa still didn't meet my eyes.

I gripped the spoon but I didn't take any cereal. I could see it getting soggy in the bowl. "Maybe I'm just happy to see you," I said. I didn't say it warmly. I said it as a challenge.

"I'm happy to see you, too," Marissa murmured. "But maybe tonight you could find somewhere else to be so that my friends and I—"

I wanted to smash the cereal bowl in her face. But instead, I said, "No problem. Don't worry about it. If I'm still at home when your friends arrive, I'll stay in the basement. I really want to finish up my cabinet."

Marissa pushed her chair back from the table and

stood up. "Thanks. Tomorrow you and I will go some-where, just the two of us. Maybe shopping?" Her tight smile lasted for only a few seconds.

Did she think I was a two-year-old? She seriously thought she could bribe me to stay away from her and her friends?

I dropped the spoon into the bowl, scraped my chair back, and stomped out of the room. Of course I was hurt and angry. But I was also confused. Why did she need me away from her friends? She didn't want to hurt me, I could see that. She just wanted me to stay away.

Why?

From Aiden?

Was that it? Could she see that I was attracted to him? Did I stand too close to him, talk to him too much, laugh at his lame jokes? Enjoy myself too much while he was there?

Marissa is a very smart girl. And she's very intuitive. She sees things. Had she seen *that*?

My emotions were swirling around my head. Yes, I felt hurt and angry. But I felt embarrassed, too. Embar-rassed that I'd acted foolishly with Aiden. Embarrassed that Marissa could see through me so effortlessly.

* * *

So that night when Marissa's friends began to arrive, I crept up to the secret attic room at the top of our house. I pulled out a spell book I had used before.

Yes, a spell book. I'm a Fear. Dark sides and weirdness are our birthright.

I lit the black candles I kept in a circle on the floor. And I chanted a few words, reading them carefully from the old book.

I didn't do anything terrible or dangerous. I just gave Marissa a very bad case of hiccups.

I was careful. I used a weak spell. It would last for only an hour or so.

I admit it. I laughed to myself. I knew Marissa would try every remedy. And her friends would keep suggesting cure after ridiculous cure. And, of course, there *is* no cure for magic.

Back downstairs, I made sure Mom and Dad weren't nearby. I stole a half-empty bottle of whiskey that no one would notice missing. I listened to the voices from the den. I recognized Marissa's friends Taylor and Dani. I heard a loud hiccup. I'm so evil, it made me start laughing again.

I carried the bottle down to my basement workshop, along with my anger and my hurt and my disbelief that Marissa could treat me like that. Like some kind of mangy family pet, banished when the company was around.

The sweet smell of the cherrywood lumber usually calmed me, delighted me, and brought my senses to life. But not tonight. I took a swig right from the bottle before I started to saw a couple of shelf boards down to size.

My uncle Kenny is usually a pain. But when he heard I was into woodwork, he sent over a ten-inch table saw and a nice-sized table drill press. They were left over from the tool warehouse Kenny had owned, until he ran it into the ground like all his other businesses.

I tried to force my angry thoughts away as I moved a three-quarter-inch square of cherrywood through the saw blade. But even the whiskey didn't seem to be helping to calm me.

I swore as my hand slipped—and I ruined one of the sheets of wood. I should have stopped right there. I knew I should have. But when you're angry and bitter and confused and alone . . . well, you don't always think so clearly, do you?

This is all a long preview leading up to what happened. I know I'm trying to explain myself and not doing a very good job of it. So . . .

I took a break and went upstairs, wiping sawdust off

the front of my sweatshirt and jeans. I could hear Marissa and her friends in the den. They all seemed to be talking at once. Their voices rang all the way in the kitchen. I heard Marissa repeating in a high, laughing voice: "Oh my God! Oh my God!"

I crossed the hall into the kitchen—and stopped when I saw Aiden.

He had his back to me at the fridge, pulling out a bottle of beer. He wore a maroon hoodie over faded jeans and, for once, he wasn't wearing the little hat.

I stood there watching him. My head was spinning. Things were a little out of focus. Maybe I had more to drink than I remembered.

He turned when I took a few steps across the tile floor. "Oh. Hi." He has the most awesome smile. It really is like his face lights up. "I wondered where you were, Harmony."

I narrowed my eyes at him. "Did you really?" Why was I putting on that teasing voice? Hadn't I been sufficiently warned by my sister?

He waved the beer bottle toward the den. "Are you coming in with us?"

I shook my head. "No. I'm working. In the basement. On my cabinet."

"Cool," he said. "Can I see it?"

He wants to go down to the basement with me.

"Sure," I said, my heart beating a little faster. "It's . . . it's just boards." And then I blurted out, "Hey, maybe you can help me with something."

What made me say that? I'll never be able to explain it. And believe me, I've thought about it ever since.

"No problem," he said, following me to the basement door.

"I can use an extra hand on this one thing," I said. "The shelves, see."

An amused smile crossed his handsome face, just for a second, but I caught it. I narrowed my eyes at him. "You're surprised to see a girl who likes to do wood-work?"

He waved a hand. "No. Of course not." I could see my question made him uncomfortable.

"Just teasing," I said. I led the way down the stairs and across the basement to my workshop against the wall.

Aiden studied the table saw and the drill press. "Impressive," he said. "This is serious stuff." He took a deep breath. "Mmmm. Smells so good. What kind of wood?"

"Cherrywood," I said. "When I apply the finish, it'll be even darker."

He tilted the beer bottle to his mouth and took a long swig. "I like it." He set the bottle down on the floor. I could hear the girls' voices from upstairs right through the basement ceiling.

"Here's my problem," I said. I picked up one of the rectangular shelf boards and shoved it into his hands. "I'm not using nails or screws or anything—I'm going to connect the shelves to the frame with wooden dowels."

He nodded. "Nice."

"I need to drill holes for the dowels in the corners of each shelf," I explained. "Very carefully. I don't want to drill all the way through. See?"

He nodded again. "I get it. So what do you want me to do?"

I stared at him and didn't answer his question. I could feel the blood pulsing at my temples. I didn't answer. I didn't think. This is where I lost it.

I lurched forward and threw my hands around his neck. I pressed myself against the board he held in front of him. And kissed him. Not just a kiss. But a full-on passionate embrace.

Holding him tightly, I moved my lips over his and waited for him to kiss back.

TWENTY-ONE

"Uh." I made a soft, startled cry as he pulled his head back. Then he used the board to push me off him. Gently, but he still pushed.

I stood there openmouthed, heart pounding, the taste of his lips on mine. "Oh. I . . ." I felt instantly silly and then confused and surprised at myself, surprised at what I had done on not even an impulse. I just did it. As if someone had cast a spell on *me*, and I wasn't the one in control.

I could feel my face go hot and I knew I must be beet red.

I've been impulsive before, especially when guys have been involved. And, believe me, it wasn't the first time I made the first move.

But I'd never been so *wrong*.

I cared about Marissa. I would never try to start a family fight. A battle over tall, blond Aiden. No. No, I wouldn't.

But there we were gazing at each other. Talk about awkward. And what did I want? I only wanted to kiss him again.

Finally, I felt I could talk. I forced a laugh. "Sorry," I said. "Just had to get that out of my system." *I can make a joke out of it.* "Welcome to the family," I said.

That made him smile. "Your sister warned me about you," he said.

I couldn't keep the surprise off my face. "Seriously? What did she say? That I'm a slut? That I'm crazy? That I'm jealous of her?"

He shrugged. "I'm not saying." His eyes kind of twinkled. Like it was all a big joke to him.

He picked up the beer bottle and drank again, his eyes on me. "Harmony, do you really want me to help you?"

"Yes." I took the shelf from him. "I need you to hold this steady."

He stared at it. "Hold it?"

"I need to drill four holes in the corners. For the dowels. But my drill press table is only twenty inches. The board doesn't fit on the table."

I tugged him over to the drill press. I held the shelf over the table to show him. "So I just need you to hold it in place."

He ran his fingers over the drill bit. "Isn't this too big?"

I shook my head. "It's a quarter-inch drill bit," I said. "The dowels will fit snugly inside the holes."

Aiden seemed to have forgotten my crazy kiss ever happened. But I still felt jittery, light-headed. I wondered if he would tell Marissa about it later.

If he did, I'd be dead meat.

He finished the beer and set the bottle down on the floor. "Harmony, how many shelves do you want to do?" he asked.

"Just two," I said. "I know you want to get back upstairs. It won't take long. Really."

He gave me that smile again. "Let's do it."

I powered up the drill. The bit made a high, shrill whirring sound and then, as it reached full speed, sent out a steady hum.

I slid the shelf upside down onto the drill press table. I moved it in place. I used a tape measure to measure the distance from the edge of the board. Then I lowered the drill bit halfway, testing the location. Yes. I had the right spot.

"Aiden, hold it steady here. By the edge," I said. I scooted to the left to make room for him.

He stepped beside me and carefully grabbed the board by the edges with both hands.

Slowly, I lowered the whirring drill bit to the shelf. Turning the dial, I moved it down half an inch, then half an inch. I gritted my teeth as the bit dug into the wood. I was determined not to let it cut all the way through. That would ruin a perfectly good shelf.

I raised the bit and blew the wood dust from the hole. Perfect.

"One down," I said.

He helped me turn the board on the drill table. I adjusted it carefully, measuring again to make sure the hole would go in the right place.

I turned the power back on, and the drill bit began to whir. Slowly, I lowered it toward the corner of the board.

And this was when it happened. This was it. And you have to believe me—*please* believe me—it was an accident. I never would have done it deliberately.

An accident, I swear. A horrible accident that I see again and again in my dreams.

As I lowered the whirring drill bit, I tripped—on the empty beer bottle, I think. I tripped and my stomach bumped the board. And Aiden's hand . . . his right hand . . . it shot forward.

I saw it. I saw the drill bit dig into the back of his hand. The bit tore into the back of Aiden's hand and buzzed *right through his hand*. The bit drilled into the back of his hand and poked out through his palm.

And before he could even scream, a spray of bright red blood splashed over me, over my face, over the front of my shirt. And the blood spun out in a wide circle, a circle of glistening red. I saw red petals like a flower. I saw a pinwheel of blood.

I guess I went crazy. And then Aiden's shrill wail broke into my daze. Howling like an injured animal, he snapped his hand free of the drill bit. I could see the hole in his palm. I could see the blood and the veins inside his hand. And his flesh . . . it looked like raw meat.

And now we both were screaming. And the blood wouldn't stop. Aiden was squeezing his hand shut with his other hand. But the blood oozed everywhere. And our screams rang off the ceiling. Shock and horror and blood. That's what I remember.

It was an accident. A horrible accident.

The hole went right through his hand. But it wasn't my fault. I swear. I swear.

But I know I'll never force that picture from my mind. Never get over the shock . . . and horror . . . and blood.

TWENTY-TWO

Two days later, Marissa and I went to see Aiden. He was staying with his cousin Shawn at an apartment in the Old Village. I had to drive because Marissa was still sobbing, mopping at tears running down her cheeks.

It was a gray April day, low clouds threatening rain. Gloomy and depressing, which fit our mood perfectly. I had to concentrate hard on my driving. I still felt shaky from the horror that night in my basement.

"You spoke to Aiden this morning after he left the hospital? What did he say?" I asked.

Marissa hadn't been talking to me. But in the car, with just the two of us, I hoped she would forget her anger and start again.

I knew she'd probably never forgive me. But if only

she would talk to me . . .

"His hand . . . ," she started in a trembling voice. "The tendons were all torn. They tried to reattach them. But . . . but they don't know if he'll be able to move his fingers again."

More tears. She dabbed at them with her wadded-up Kleenex.

"Oh my God," I murmured. A fresh wave of guilt washed over me. I lost my concentration. The car slid to the right. I had to jerk the wheel hard to get back in the lane. "Marissa—I'm so sorry . . ."

"Stop saying you're sorry," Marissa snapped, her jaw clenched.

"But—"

"You ruined Aiden's life," she said, her eyes burning into mine. "He'll never be a surgeon if he can't use his fingers."

"I know, but maybe—"

"You're trying to ruin *my* life—aren't you?" Now she was screaming. Her voice shrill in the small car. *"Aren't you?"*

"No. Of course not!" I protested. "You've got to believe me. It was a total accident. I tripped. It's the truth."

She didn't reply. She crossed her arms in front of her

and glared out the window, her face twisted in anger.

I made the turn onto Division Street, a little too fast, but I kept control even though my hands were cold and shaking. "You're never going to believe me—are you?" I said in a tiny voice. "You're never going to forgive me?"

She didn't move and didn't answer. Kept her arms wrapped tightly around her and stared out the windshield, her expression stone hard, her mouth set in a furious scowl.

And suddenly, my sorrow, my guilt, my shame . . . it all faded away. I could feel it wash away, as if I was getting lighter, floating, rising above it.

And then I felt a deep surge of red anger raging up from the pit of my stomach. Anger so powerful that I had an urge to crush the gas pedal and slam the car into a wall.

We are sisters, I thought. *Why can't we ever stick together as a family? Why does Marissa resent me so much? Why does she hate me? Why can't she forgive me?*

And as I pulled the car into a narrow parking space in front of the apartment building, my anger led me to darker thoughts:

You should be nicer to me, Marissa. You don't know the things I can do.

* * *

I don't know anything about the visit with Aiden. Even though I was desperate to see him and tell him how sorry I was, Marissa made me wait in the car.

When she returned after about twenty minutes, she was pale and shaken. She refused to say a word to me.

That night, a bunch of Marissa's friends came over to console her. Her best friend, Taylor, squeezed next to her on the big armchair in the den and kept her arm draped around Marissa's shoulders. Olivia and Dani were there, too.

They all spoke in near whispers, and there was a lot of head shaking and sorrowful frowns, and muttering. I could hear Taylor talking about the screams they heard that night from the basement. "It sounded like a wild animal. Seriously. I was so terrified. I thought a wolf or something had crawled into your basement. I had no idea it was Aiden."

She wasn't doing a very good job of cheering Marissa up. None of them were.

Of course, I wasn't allowed in the room. Marissa had made that very clear to me. That afternoon, I eavesdropped on a conversation she had with Mom.

Marissa told Mom that Aiden was out of his mind

with anger. He couldn't stop screaming and waving his hand with the huge cast on it, threatening her with it. Marissa said he blamed our whole family. He kept saying he was going to sue us.

Mom isn't good in situations like this. She gets so defensive, she doesn't think straight. "I thought there was something wrong with that boy from the moment you brought him in," I heard her say.

Marissa went ballistic. "Something *wrong* with him? Mom, you can't blame Aiden. How can you blame Aiden? Harmony destroyed his hand. Harmony ruined his life!"

"Don't say that," Mom replied. "Don't say that about your sister. Did you see how devastated she was?"

"Ha!" Marissa cried. "Devastated? Mom, Harmony—"

"You're always trying to blame people. You know it was an accident."

"I *don't* know it," Marissa insisted.

Listening in the hall, her words gave me a deep shudder. How could Marissa think I did it deliberately?

She really hates me, that's how.

Now it was after dinner—our silent dinner. Dad was away on a business trip. Mom tried to start a conversation a few times. But Marissa and I muttered replies to our dinner plates. And Robby remained silent. Mom gave up and we ate in total silence. The clink of our forks on the plates never sounded so loud.

It was as if someone had died. Like a funeral in our house. And when Marissa's friends showed up, it didn't get any cheerier.

Since Marissa made it clear I wasn't allowed in the room, I listened outside the den door. I didn't have anything else to do. For a moment, I considered going downstairs and working on my cabinet.

I had cleaned up all the blood, although the floor was still stained. But it didn't matter. I think I realized somewhere in the back of my mind that I'd never work down there again.

"Hey—!" I cried out as something bumped me in the back.

I turned and saw Mom. She held an oval tray of blondies in both hands. "A snack for them," she said, whispering for some reason. "Bring it in to them."

Mom makes the best blondies in America. Believe me, I wanted to eat the whole tray. But I obediently pushed open the den door and carried in the tray.

I saw Marissa's expression change immediately.

Her eyes flashed with anger.

"From Mom," I said.

"Set it down on the coffee table, and leave," Marissa snapped.

I could see the surprise on Taylor's face.

But I didn't want to argue or anything. I set the tray down, wheeled around, and strode from the room. As I pulled the den door nearly closed, I saw all of them reaching for the blondies.

I shut my eyes and whispered a spell, a few words I had memorized from one of the old books. I knew I shouldn't be doing what I was doing. But Marissa's anger had rubbed off on me.

Then I leaned against the wall, just out of sight, and listened. Marissa's three friends all talked about how sorry they felt for her. And I heard Marissa tell them that she would never forgive me. A chill ran down my back, and something snapped inside me. I mean, why would a sister say that to her friends?

I should have gone up to my room or out of the house. Standing there, listening to Marissa's hatred, only made me feel weak and sad. But I couldn't leave the doorway. I was waiting for Doug to arrive.

I knew Doug would spark a little life into the evening.

That's why I called him that afternoon and invited him over.

When I spoke to him, he was totally surprised to learn that Marissa was in town. That meant she hadn't found the courage to break up with him yet. So . . . both Doug and my sister were in for a big surprise.

And when Doug came bursting into the den, so big and broad, like a bull as always . . . When Doug came bursting in, the girls all gasped and cried out, and did a terrible job of hiding their surprise.

Doug left the den door wide open, so I could see the whole thing. Doug stood in the middle of the room, looking like the Hulk, staring hard at Marissa, who still shared the armchair with Taylor.

"Marissa." Doug was breathing hard, as if he'd run all the way to our house. "You didn't tell me you were in town." He managed to sound hurt and angry at the same time.

Marissa squeezed past Taylor and struggled to her feet. "I . . . well . . . I'm sorry. It was a short visit and—"

Marissa is not a good liar. You have to be quick to lie well. That just isn't how her mind works.

Taylor jumped up and scrambled beside Dani on the couch. Olivia sat cross-legged on the carpet beside the couch. All three of them looked as if they'd love to be somewhere else.

"I've been texting you," Doug said. He shoved back the hood of his gray hoodie.

"I know," Marissa said. Her cheeks were bright pink.

Doug squinted at her. "Is something wrong?"

Marissa shook her head. From the doorway, I saw tears bubble in her eyes. "No. Well . . . yes. I mean—"

Was Marissa going to tell Doug about Aiden? Was she going to break up with him right in front of her friends?

Doug curled his big hands into fists, then uncurled them. He shifted his weight from right to left. "I don't get it."

Marissa started toward him. "We need to talk. But not now."

He backed away from her. "You mean—?"

"It just happened, Doug," Marissa blurted out. "I didn't mean for it to. But . . ."

From the doorway, I saw Doug's face darken, almost to purple. "What are you saying? I don't understand."

Marissa's three friends shifted uncomfortably. Could this be more embarrassing? Marissa was breaking Doug's heart, and they were, like, in the audience watching.

Marissa avoided Doug's stare. "I . . . met someone else," she said in a whisper.

Doug nodded. His eyes went blank. Even from a distance, I could see he was trying to process her words.

He rubbed his hand back through his hair. He shifted his weight again. "You . . . you promised. Didn't you promise?"

"It just happened, Doug," Marissa said, her eyes still on the floor.

"Happened." Doug muttered the word. His face was still purple, his expression a blank. "Happened."

Then he swung his big body around and stomped out of the room without another word. He brushed past me, bumping me out of the doorway. A few seconds later, the front door slammed hard.

Marissa stood in the center of the den, her back to her friends, her silent friends. She hugged herself and made a shivering sound. "I see you there, Harmony," she said in a cold voice I barely recognized. "Come . . . in . . . here."

I took a deep breath and stepped into the doorway, but I didn't enter the room.

Marissa pointed a shaky finger at me. "You called Doug, didn't you? Don't even answer. I know you did. I know you called him."

I didn't move and I didn't reply.

"Stay out of my life," Marissa said through clenched teeth. "I mean it. You are ruining everything for me. What is your problem?"

"Marissa—?" Taylor tried to interrupt. I think she'd had enough drama for one night. Or maybe she just wanted a chance to calm Marissa down.

Marissa ignored her and kept her furious expression on me. "Look at you, Harmony. Messing with *my* boyfriends. Messing with my life. Look at you. What are you wearing? Those are my old clothes, the clothes I left behind when I left for Wisconsin."

I was breathing hard, feeling dizzy from the anger pouring off my sister.

"Do you want to *be* me—is that it, Harmony?" Marissa screamed. "You really want to *be* me?"

"Marissa, stop—" Taylor tried again.

But a hoarse groan made everyone turn around.

Another throaty groan, and Olivia bent her head and vomited loudly onto the carpet.

"What's wrong? Are you sick?" Dani cried, jumping to her feet. And then Dani's eyes rolled up, and she grabbed her stomach. She took two staggering steps forward. Then she threw up all over the couch.

I stepped back from the doorway. All four of them were vomiting now, holding their stomachs, bent in two, and loudly spitting up big puddles of yellow and brown.

I spun away so they wouldn't see me smile.

I'm so bad. But that incantation was just so, so good.

TWENTY-THREE

That all happened a little over a year ago. The memories came flooding back, I guess, because they were never really far from my mind. A year later, I still woke up in a cold sweat, my recurring dream of Aiden screaming, his blood splashing everywhere, the dream lingering, still filling me with horror and regret.

Marissa and I barely spoke after that. She went back to school, and stayed in Wisconsin all summer, taking a few courses, enjoying the new friends she had made there.

She told my parents that Aiden never came back to school. He just vanished without a word to her. She tried to track him down, just to see if his hand was healing, just to apologize one more time, but she had no luck.

Marissa didn't come home until Thanksgiving.

She seemed the same, except that she had gained ten pounds. I guess that's what people do in college. She blamed it on Wisconsin, all the beer and cheese.

She was still beautiful, of course. Still talented and beautiful. She played a flute sonata for Mom and Dad that was spectacular. She let me listen from the back of the room.

She still was barely speaking to me. Just "good morning" or "good night." She never asked me a question about my life or my year, never tried to start a conversation.

Okay. I get it. I'd done a terrible thing. But it was time for Marissa to get over it. I had no idea how to win her over or break through the icy barrier she had built between us.

That winter break, she got back with Doug. It seemed only natural. And they made plans to get married. I knew it was at Doug's urging. He was desperate to make sure another Aiden wouldn't come along.

Doug was assistant manager at the furniture store now, and still taking courses toward a business degree. But I just didn't think he was right for Marissa.

She was so artistic and talented and social. She needed

to be surrounded by friends all the time. Doug's idea of a good night was staying home, having a few beers, and watching whatever was on ESPN.

My parents instantly got involved in arranging the wedding, reserving the lodge, figuring out the invitation list, and all the other hundred things you have to do to organize a big deal like that. It seemed to me they immersed themselves in the project so they didn't have to consider whether the marriage was a good thing for Marissa or not.

But that was *my* take on it.

I don't remember a conversation in which my parents gave an opinion on the subject of Doug. Or even made a single remark about him. They just seemed to accept him as an inevitability. As if it was only natural. And, of course, they really didn't have a choice in the matter.

Robby and I had a few short conversations about Doug. But by winter, Robby was obsessed with Nikki, and it was hard to get him to talk about anything else.

I was worried about him. Nikki was his first girlfriend, and he was completely out-of-his-mind crazy about her. And I hoped he wasn't about to get hurt. He was up so high, the trip down would be a disaster.

Robby liked Doug. They were kind of pals. They

spent hours in Robby's room playing *Halo Wars 2* and *Call of Duty: Black Ops.*

When Marissa was home on a break and Doug stayed for dinner, he and Robby discussed their games the whole time. And Marissa would roll her eyes and beg them to stop.

I knew video games bored her to tears.

With Marissa and Doug, I saw only problems. And I knew there was little I could do about it, because my sister and I had become so distant, with miles of anger and hurt between us.

The wedding plans went fine. I wasn't really involved. No one asked me to help out with anything. It all went smoothly—until my parents announced to Robby that Nikki wasn't on the guest list.

He went ballistic, of course. Exploded. He screamed and begged and pleaded and acted like your basic ten-year-old. And when his tantrums didn't work, he threatened to stay home and skip the wedding.

No way he'd get away with that. But believe me, there were a lot of silent meals and slammed doors in my house. Robby spent more and more time at Nikki's.

I spent a lot of time in the little attic room. I was eager to learn new magic. And it was a good escape from everything happening in my house.

I'd found a chapter on mind-control spells in one of the dusty old books. They were complicated and confusing, and I wondered if I was ready to perform any of them.

I felt bad for Robby, and I had the crazy idea that I could use one of the spells on Mom and Dad and make them change their minds about inviting Nikki.

At dinner one night, just the three of us, Dad's favorite—spaghetti and sausage—on the table, I shut my eyes and concentrated on the spell. The spaghetti steamed on my face as I focused on the ancient words.

The spell required tremendous mind power. I practically had to go into a trance for my silent chant to work.

"Harmony? Are you okay?" Mom's voice penetrated my concentration.

I ignored her and struggled to go deeper into my mind.

Please work. . . . Please work. . . .

When I opened my eyes, they were both staring at me. Dad was the first to grab his forehead. Then Mom uttered a gasp and began to rub her temples.

"I suddenly have such a splitting headache," Mom groaned.

"Me too," Dad said. "Is the spaghetti too hot?"

I had succeeded only in giving them both headaches.

The spell was a horrible flop. I realized I wasn't ready for the hard stuff. No way my feeble magic could help Robby.

So here we are. It's June, a year after the whole Aiden thing. One whole year later. Tomorrow Marissa and Doug will be husband and wife.

I've had my fun. I played my little feather and squirrel tricks. I got back at Marissa for not making me maid of honor, or even including me in the wedding.

Taylor will be up there with her, and I'll be sitting beside Robby and my parents. And I'm going to behave from now on, I swear. I'm just going to let it all play out.

So, the night before the big affair, I took a walk in the sweet fresh air, following the path through the flowers and the tall, fragrant grass.

And I knew I saw Aiden, with the little hat and the long strides, Aiden stepping out of the red sports car and moving like Aiden, leaning forward as if eager to get somewhere. I recognized him even in the shadows of the lodge parking lot.

But I didn't believe my eyes. I hurried to my room to think about it all. I thought I was having some kind of flashback. Because Aiden didn't belong here. Aiden was a horror story from a year ago, long gone, long banished to my nightmares.

Seeing him brought the nightmares back. And then I had a flash. I jumped up from my bed. It finally dawned on me that I could just call his room. Or maybe even go talk to him.

If it really *was* Aiden.

I returned to the front desk. A slender middle-aged man in a gray suit appeared from the back office, carrying a stack of files. He had straight, slicked-back black hair, dark eyes, and a serious expression.

I leaned on the counter and waited for him to set the files down. I wasn't sure he had seen me. The brass name tag on his jacket read *Akira Himuro*. "Mr. Himuro?" I called.

He turned and put on a professional smile. "How can I help you?"

"I need to find a friend," I said. "His name is Aiden Murray."

Mr. Himuro stepped to the counter and typed some keys on the computer behind the desk. He nodded. "Yes. Mr. Aiden Murray."

"Could you tell me his room number?" I asked.

"Oh, I am so sorry," he replied. "Hotel policy. I'm

not allowed to give room numbers. It's a privacy thing, you know."

"I know," I said, tapping my fingers tensely on the countertop. "But . . . well . . . He's a member of the wedding party. And I really have to get a message to him."

Okay. I lied. I'm good at it. Sue me.

He gazed at the computer monitor and shook his head. "I'm so sorry. Company policy, you know." He pointed to a telephone at the other end of the counter. "Just use the house phone. The operator will connect you to Mr. Murray, and he can tell you his room number."

"Okay. Thanks," I said.

"I hope you enjoy the wedding," he said. "It's supposed to be sunny and warm tomorrow."

"Thank you," I repeated.

I heard a musical ringtone. Mr. Himuro pulled a phone from his pants pocket. He raised it to his ear and walked off toward the back office.

As soon as he was out of sight, I spread both hands on the counter edge and hoisted myself onto the counter. Stretching my neck, I could read his computer monitor. I quickly saw he had left it on Aiden's page.

Aiden Murray. Room 237.

Thirty seconds later, I stood outside Aiden's door. I

raised my fist three times to knock, but pulled my hand down each time. Maybe it would have been easier to talk to him on the phone. But I wanted to see his face when he told me what he was doing here.

My throat was suddenly dry. My hands were cold. I took a deep breath and finally managed to knock. "Aiden?"

I heard someone moving in there, walking to the door. "Yes. Who is it?"

"Aiden? It's me. Harmony Fear."

The door swung open. But just a crack. Just enough for him to stick his head out. "Harmony? Oh, hey." He eyed me up and down.

He looked the same. Same scruff on his face. Same tousled, curly blond hair. He wore a T-shirt with the name of a band on it I'd never heard of, over tight dark jeans.

"Can I come in?" I asked, my voice trembling just a little.

He shrugged. "What for?"

That was cold.

I suddenly had a bad feeling about this conversation.

"What are you doing here?" I blurted out.

Why not come right to the point?

He stood blocking my view of the room behind him, the door only a little bit open. "No reason," he said. His face was a blank. I couldn't read his expression at all. I had the feeling someone was in the room with him, but I couldn't see past him.

"Excuse me? You're here for no reason?"

"I'm just here, Harmony. That's all." He made sure I could see he was annoyed by the question.

"That makes no sense at all," I said.

"I know."

"Why are you being so mysterious, Aiden?"

"I'm not. I told you. I'm just here."

"For the wedding tomorrow?"

"No. Not really."

This conversation was ridiculous.

"Are you still angry about your hand?" I asked. "Is that why you're being so weird?"

"I'm not being weird."

"Well, how *is* your hand?"

"Not great. But it's getting better," he said. Then he added, "Slowly."

"So, come on, Aiden. Tell me. Why did you come to Marissa's wedding?"

He just stared at me.

"To cause trouble?" I said. "To interfere? To wish her well? To see her one more time? To toast the happy couple?"

His eyes burned into mine. "Harmony, I'm sorry. I *really* don't want to talk to you."

He didn't slam the door. But he closed it so hard the doorframe shook.

TWENTY-FOUR

The irresistible smell of bacon led me to the breakfast room. The room was enormous, like a summer camp mess hall with rows of wooden picnic tables and benches, and a long buffet serving table at the back.

I was still half awake, yawning and rubbing the sleep from my eyes. I saw the line of guests moving slowly along the buffet table, piling scrambled eggs, breakfast potatoes, bacon and sausage onto their plates.

The clinks of plates and glasses and coffee cups and the ringing blare of voices helped to wake me up. I focused my eyes and, stepping into the room, searched for Aiden.

No sign of him.

Uncle Kenny waved to me from a table at the near end of a row. Max was perched on his knees on the picnic bench across from Kenny. He had a big stack of pancakes on his plate.

Kenny must have cut the pancakes into pieces for Max. The kid was dunking the pieces into syrup, eating them with his hands. I had to laugh. His fingers were dripping with syrup, and he had somehow smeared it over one cheek.

Marissa's friends Taylor and Dani were at the next table, bowls of yogurt and fruit in front of them. They waved to me and I waved back. I didn't feel like eating. I just needed about a gallon of coffee.

I was desperate to tell Robby that Aiden was here. But he was against the far wall, his table crowded with guys I didn't recognize, probably Doug's friends.

A loud crash made me jump. Someone had dropped a plate of eggs. The plate shattered as the eggs spilled over the floor in the middle of the buffet line. Two white-uniformed attendants bent to gather it all up.

I found the coffee dispenser and filled a white mug to the brim. I love the smell of coffee. The aroma wakes me up before I even drink it.

Gripping the mug between my hands, I spotted an

empty place at my parents' table near the center of the room. I nodded good morning to them as I lowered myself onto the bench.

Mom was red-eyed and the lines beneath her eyes appeared darker than usual. She wore a blue wool cap over her hair. She had a bowl of oatmeal and strawberries in front of her, but had barely touched it.

"Did you sleep?" I asked. She's a terrible sleeper.

"Not much. I kept thinking of all the things that could go wrong today."

I laughed. Typical Mom. "Why didn't you think about *happy* things? You know. Things that could go *right*?"

Her turn to laugh. "Does that sound like me?"

Mom has a good sense of humor about herself. Usually, she's hyper-serious. She can be intense. She went to law school, even though she never practiced, and she has a lawyer's eye for details. And she loves to argue.

I don't think I've ever won an argument with her. Even if she knows she's wrong, she will outlast you. Marissa gets along much better with Mom than I do. She can be as intense and argumentative as Mom.

I'm not like that. Mom and I have had some pretty big fights. Sometimes they get very emotional. Sometimes there's a lot of anger between us.

So I guess my favorite thing about my mom is that she can make jokes about herself, and she doesn't get all worked up if you tease her.

I couldn't decide whether or not to tell my parents about seeing Aiden. *Maybe they already know he's here*, I thought. And then before I could decide what to do, my dad started clinking his orange juice glass with the handle of his spoon, and he jumped to his feet, nearly knocking over his coffee mug.

"A toast!" He had to shout really loud because the din of voices rang off the walls and the low rafters. "A breakfast toast!"

The big room seemed to settle down in waves, first one table, then the next, stretching to the far wall. Dad raised his orange juice glass. Was it a mimosa? Was he already celebrating with champagne in his juice? I couldn't tell.

"A good-morning toast to the bride and groom!" he boomed.

Some people raised glasses, some coffee mugs. I heard Max yell, "More syrup! I want more syrup!"

"Good morning, everyone," Dad said. "We are already blessed with a beautiful day of sun and blue skies for our wedding on the mesa."

Some guys at Robby's table cheered. I saw that Robby already had his phone to his ear.

"Before we all head out," my dad continued, "and get ourselves dressed and looking our finest for the big event, I wanted to say a quick salute to the bride and groom."

He glanced around the room. "Well, I see our bride has not come down yet, so I will offer my thanks to the lucky groom." He turned toward Doug.

To my surprise, Doug was sitting all by himself at a table near the doors. *Why isn't he sitting with his friends?* I wondered. He looked as if he'd been at the bar all night. His hair was down over his face. His black-and-red Metallica T-shirt was ripped at the collar.

"A simple toast," Dad continued, his voice echoing off the rafters. "I just want to say thank you. Thank you, Doug, and thank you, Marissa, for giving us all a reason to come together at this beautiful resort and celebrate!" He raised his glass higher. "Thank you both!"

Raised glasses and the words *thank you* repeated around the room. Dad sat down with a smile on his face. He turned to Mom. "Guess our daughter is taking the whole beauty rest thing seriously. She's going to miss breakfast."

"Marissa never eats breakfast anyway," I reminded

him. "That's how she keeps her perfect figure, remember?"

Dad frowned at me. "Harmony, you're not being sarcastic, are you? Please don't be sarcastic on your sister's wedding day."

I kissed his forehead. "Dad, I don't have a sarcastic bone in my body. You know that."

I jumped up and, carrying my coffee mug, made my way to Doug's table. He had his elbows on the table and was resting his head in his hands. He didn't smile as I approached. I realized I hadn't seen him smile much the whole weekend.

I dropped down across from him. "What's your problem?" I don't like to beat around the bush.

He stirred as if I'd awoken him. "Excuse me?"

"You okay?" I asked, squinting hard at him. He hadn't shaved yet. One eye was a lot redder than the other. "You're sitting here by yourself?"

He shrugged. "Resting up, you know?"

I took a long sip of coffee. "Shouldn't you be broing around with your buddies? You know. Happy groom stuff."

He stared back at me, still without smiling. "I guess."

"Come on, Doug," I said. "What's wrong?"

"Nothing. Give me a break, Harmony. I'm just tense, you know. Don't I have a right to be nervous?"

I didn't know how to answer that. "Sorry," I muttered. I started to get up.

"No worries." He forced a smile. Even his smile was kind of grim. Like it was painful for him. *He's such a sullen guy*, I thought. And for the thousandth time I thought, *What does Marissa see in him?*

I decided maybe I did need some breakfast. The wedding was scheduled for one o'clock. There wouldn't be a chance to eat until the reception afterward.

I was nearly to the food table when someone grabbed my legs and nearly tackled me to the floor. I twisted around. "Max! Hey! Let go, buddy! Let go!"

He tossed back his head and laughed. He tightened his arms around my legs.

"Sorry." Uncle Kenny had to pry the little monster off me. "Max is excited about the wedding," Kenny said. "Aren't you, Max?"

"No." He burst forward to tackle me again, but Kenny managed to restrain him.

"Max, tell Harmony what you're going to do at the wedding," Uncle Kenny urged.

"Throw flowers," Max said.

I laughed. "Yes. You're the flower boy. You carry the basket of flowers at the end of the line."

"I'm going to throw them," Max said.

"Wait till you see Max in his tux," Kenny said, patting him on the shoulder.

"No tux," Max shouted. "No tux!"

"Shhhh." Kenny patted the kid's shoulder some more.

"I can't believe they don't have omelets," Kenny said. "A place like this, they should have their own omelet chef, don't you think? The scrambled eggs were so cold, they were probably right out of the freezer."

"That's too bad," I murmured. What could I say? I watched Max lead Kenny out of the dining hall. *Guess I won't have the scrambled eggs*, I decided.

I don't know where the rest of the morning went. I guess I spent the whole time getting ready for the wedding. A new makeup and hair guy arrived a little after ten. I usually don't like people fussing over me. I refuse to ever get a massage. It just makes me uncomfortable.

But I liked this guy, mostly because he was fast. He kept telling me what beautiful eyes I have. Such a liar. I know my eyes are pale and kind of dull, not my best feature. But he was trying to be nice, so I didn't call him on it.

He put a lot of product on my hair. He said it was windy at the top of the mesa, and he didn't want my hair to blow away. Then he did some nice things with eyeliner that made me look more dramatic, and gave me a lipstick much darker than I'd ever used. It was actually a good look for me.

My dress was simple and *not lilac*. Marissa had picked lilac for all the dresses the girls in her wedding party wore. For once, I was glad I was going to be an innocent bystander.

My dress was red. Long and simple and not sexy enough to take away from Marissa. But it was red, and I expected a few comments about it.

I was just adjusting the top when Robby burst into my room without knocking. "How do you do this?" he cried. "Harmony, do you know how to do this?"

He waved a black tuxedo bow tie in my face.

He was in a white tuxedo shirt, ruffled in the front, and tuxedo pants with wide suspenders that made him look ridiculous. Thank goodness the jacket would cover them.

"Are you going to wear a cummerbund?" I asked.

"I don't think that came with the tux," he said. "I don't really know what it is anyway." He pushed the bow tie at me. "How am I supposed to know how to tie this?"

"How am *I* supposed to know?" I replied. I took it and dangled it in front of me. "Robby, it's a man thing, you know?"

He grabbed it back. "You've *got* to know. You're supposed to know things."

I laughed. "Is that a compliment?" I pulled him toward the door. "Dad will know how to tie it," I said. "Come on. Let's ask him."

Robby pulled back. "I don't know. I heard them fighting in their room. Mom was screaming at him."

"About what?"

"I couldn't hear."

"Why does everyone get so weirded out before a wedding?" I asked, mainly to myself. I pulled open the door. "Come on. Let's break up the fight and get Dad to tie your tie."

So we walked down the hall to their room at the very end. A white-uniformed woman pushed a cart past us, the shelves loaded with trays of cookies and small pastries. I wanted to grab a few off the cart, but I restrained myself.

Robby and I nodded to two of Marissa's friends, their lilac dresses down almost to the floor, as we passed. "You look gorgeous!" I told them.

Robby and I stepped up to our parents' door. Silence

in their room. The fight must have ended, I hoped in a draw.

I raised my hand to knock—and the door swung open.

Mom poked her head out. Her hair was up, shiny, and I'm sure sprayed just as stiff as mine. She was still in a white hotel bathrobe.

"Go help your sister," she said before Robby and I could say anything.

"What's her problem?" Robby said.

"There's no one helping her," Mom said. She sounded breathless. I could see she was in a panic. "She's all alone down there. I don't understand it."

"Did you talk to her?" I asked.

"No. She doesn't answer her phone. She didn't come down to breakfast. I can't reach her."

"Weird," I muttered.

"Just go," Mom said. "Go help her. I don't know if her friends are with her or not. She needs help to get dressed and everything."

"Okay," I said. "I'll see what I can do."

"What can I do?" Robby said. "I can't help her. I need help with this stupid thing." He waved the bow tie in Mom's face.

"Okay. You go, Harmony. Help her. Call me on my cell if you need me. I'll be dressed in another ten minutes."

She stepped back so Robby could enter the room. The door closed. I stood there for a few seconds. *Why weren't Marissa's friends helping her? Taylor? Dani? Olivia and the others?*

"Sisters should help sisters," I muttered mockingly. I turned left at the end of the hall and hurried to Marissa's suite at the far end. I felt the worn carpet under my feet, and I realized I hadn't even put my heels on yet.

I reached Marissa's door, took a deep breath, and raised my hand to knock. "Marissa?" I called, pressing my face close to the door. "It's me."

No reply.

I knocked three times, pretty hard knocks. "I came to help you, Marissa," I called. "Do you need help?"

Still no reply.

I pressed my ear against the door and listened. I couldn't hear any movement in there, no footsteps, no music on, nothing.

"Hey, Marissa?" My voice got shrill. "Open up. Come on. Mom said I should help you."

Silence.

I grabbed the brass doorknob. Turned it and pushed. The door swung open. "Marissa? Hey—!" I stepped through the short entryway. The suite opened to a living room on the right, the bedroom to the left.

Marissa's wedding dress was draped over the back of the leather living room couch.

"Marissa?"

I turned and strode to the bedroom. The bed was made. It looked as if it hadn't been slept in. No clothes strewn about. No cosmetics bag in the bathroom.

My heart starting to pound, I slid open the closet door. The closet was empty.

My throat tightened. I had to remember to breathe normally.

"Marissa? Hey, Marissa?"

She was gone.

I froze there for a moment, the room twirling in front of my eyes. I had to force myself to start breathing again.

This can't be happening.

And then I murmured out loud, "Get moving. You have to tell Mom and Dad."

I gripped the door handle, then stopped.

A white envelope lay at my feet. I bent to pick it up. My name was scrawled in red ink on the back.

A note for me? Did Marissa leave me a note?

I tore the envelope open with a trembling hand. I pulled out a ripped strip of yellow paper. I raised it to my face and read the words scribbled raggedly in red ink:

DON'T LOOK FOR ME

PART THREE

PART THREE

TWENTY-FIVE

"Marissa is gone. Her wedding dress is still there, but the rest of her things have been cleared out. Her bed doesn't look like it was slept in."

The words burst from my mouth in a breathless rush. They didn't even sound like words to me. I couldn't believe I was saying them.

Mom uttered a low groan and started to collapse. I saw her eyes roll up and her knees bend. Dad grabbed her and helped her into a chair.

She kept murmuring, "No no no no" and shaking her head. A single tear rolled down the makeup on one cheek.

Robby lowered his phone to his pants pocket. He

squinted at me as if he didn't recognize me. Dad held Mom's hand, his eyes on me. "You're sure?"

"She . . . isn't there," I stammered. "She's gone, Dad. You can look for yourself." I didn't mean to sound harsh, but I was having trouble breathing and I couldn't control my voice.

I wanted to scream. I wanted to cry. But my parents looked so pale and distressed, I knew I had to keep it together.

"Where's Doug?" Robby asked. "Maybe she's with Doug?"

Mom gazed up at Dad. "Do you think—?"

Robby raised his phone and punched a number. "I'll try him."

We didn't move, staring at Robby. I had my fingers crossed. *Please, please, be with Doug.*

Robby lowered his phone. "No answer."

"This is impossible," Dad muttered. "Marissa wouldn't just leave without telling anyone. That's not like her."

"Then where is she?" Mom cried.

Before anyone could answer, a knock on the door. "Come in!" I shouted.

I know we all hoped it was Marissa. But Rita

Gonzalez, the wedding planner, stepped into the room, her trusty clipboard pressed against the front of her gown.

"The guests are in place," she announced. "It's time to go out to the site. I've been looking for the bride. Do you know—" She stopped when she saw the grim expressions around the room.

She lowered the clipboard to her side. "What's wrong? Please tell me."

I spoke up first. "You haven't seen Marissa?"

"No. Not since last night. Is she dressed? Should I send my assistant for her?"

"She's gone," I said. Again, the words didn't really seem real.

Rita gave a sharp intake of breath. "Gone? You mean—?"

"I mean gone," I said. "She's not in her room, and she isn't dressed, and her stuff is missing."

Rita kind of slumped. She recovered quickly. "Cold feet, do you think?"

"We don't know what to think," I said. Dad was comforting Mom, holding on to the shoulders of her dress from the side of the chair.

Robby was on the phone again. "I keep trying

Marissa's number. It goes right to voice mail. I sent her a text, but it says undelivered."

"The guests are all seated," Rita said. "The minister arrived and is waiting to take his place at the altar."

Dad sighed. "We have to make an announcement, I guess. What can we do? We have to tell them there will be no wedding."

"I can do that for you, Mr. Fear," Rita said.

Dad thought for a moment. "No. Thank you, Ms. Gonzalez. I think I'd better do it myself."

"Is someone going to tell Doug first?" I asked.

They stared at me blankly, as if they'd all forgotten about Doug.

Robby punched Doug's number on the phone again. "He isn't picking up."

"I'm sure he's on the mesa with his best man," Rita said. "Calming his nerves before he takes his place at the altar."

"I'll go tell him," I said, starting to the door. I was suddenly desperate to get out of that room. There was no air to breathe. The shock was taking away all the oxygen.

I hurtled out the back door of the lodge. I was running on sheer nervous energy. I wanted to collapse in a heap like Mom, curl into a ball and not come out. But I knew they needed me to help handle everything.

Marissa was always their go-to person, the one they relied on. But now it had to be me.

The afternoon sun was high in a pale blue sky. The grass swayed in a soft breeze, gleaming like gold in the sunlight, as I trotted up the dirt path to the mesa top.

I could hear music as I approached, a string quartet playing some kind of light classical music. And I could hear the soft murmur of voices as our guests, seated on both sides of the red-carpeted aisle, waited for a wedding that wasn't going to happen.

As I climbed the slope toward the top, the altar came into view. It was covered in lilacs (what else?), Marissa's favorite flower. Of course, June was past lilac season. But Dad somehow had them frozen or something, shipped in for the wedding. Anything for Marissa.

Breathing hard, I trotted up the path, tall grass brushing the skirt of my dress. I spotted Doug at the back of the seats, standing by himself, his tuxedo shining in the bright sunlight, hands stuffed into his pockets. He had his head down, almost as if he were praying—and didn't see me until I rushed up to him, gasping for breath.

When I touched his shoulder, he finally raised his head. "Harmony? What's up?"

"Doug, I . . ." I struggled to get the words out. "Listen, Doug . . . I have to tell you . . ."

He narrowed his eyes at me. I could see the impatience on his face, mixed with confusion.

"Marissa is gone," I finally managed to choke out.

He didn't move. "Excuse me?"

"Marissa isn't in her room. She took her stuff. She's gone."

He blinked his eyes several times. I could see he was struggling to process it.

"She's gone," I repeated. I wasn't sure if he understood me.

A fly buzzed around his head. He made no move to brush it away.

Finally, he uttered a loud curse. When he removed his hands from his pockets, they were balled into tight fists. His eyes went wide, and his mouth formed a scowl. He cursed again.

Then he brushed past me, nearly knocking me over, and went stomping down the path toward the lodge. I stood stunned, watching him kick at the grass as he walked, tight fists at his sides.

Weird, I thought. *He didn't seem surprised at all. Did Doug know this might happen?*

I didn't have long to think about it. My dad's voice interrupted my thoughts.

I turned to see him at the altar. He had the microphone in his hand and was saying something to the minister. They were head to head, nearly touching, and I saw the minister's face go red.

Dad turned to the guests and raised the microphone to his face. "Hello, guests. I—" The loudspeaker squealed. Dad lowered the microphone a few inches.

"I have a sad announcement," he said. His voice boomed against the tall cliffs. A hush fell over the rows of guests. "I am sorry to say there will be no wedding today."

Startled cries and gasps rang out, but no one spoke.

"It seems my daughter Marissa has disappeared," Dad continued. He stood with the microphone raised, stood in silence. I think he was struggling to think of what to say next.

Finally, he lowered the microphone to its stand. He didn't say another word. He walked back down the aisle, past the startled guests, keeping his head high, eyes straight ahead, not looking at anyone. He walked right past me but I'm not sure he saw me.

And now the voices rose over the mesa as everyone jumped up, all talking at once, shaking their heads, faces tight with confusion and surprise.

I saw Max and Uncle Kenny having a heated discussion. I could see that Max was refusing to leave. He had a job as flower boy, and he wanted to do it. Kenny tugged Max's arm as he tried to explain the wedding was off. Marta, his mom, dabbed at her tears.

Aunt Dora needed help. She needed a walker, and her daughter, my cousin Nadia, seemed too preoccupied, talking to others and shaking her head, to help her mother.

I stood in the grass at the side of the path and watched people make their way to the lodge. Their expressions were all grim, showing their surprise.

I received a few sympathetic nods. But no one asked me a question or made a comment or said anything at all. I don't know why I stood there, still as a statue. I guess I was in no hurry to go back to my parents' room, back to the sadness and the shock and worry about what happened to my sister.

"Maybe she just got cold feet," I overheard my cousin Amy say as she passed by me. "I never thought that boy was right for her."

Everyone seemed to be talking at once, all in hushed tones.

"I thought this only happens in the movies."

"Couldn't she have decided to split *before* we paid all

that money to fly out here?"

"Poor girl. I can't imagine what she's going through right now."

"So many bad omens . . ."

I turned to see who was saying that. It was Marissa's friend Olivia. She was walking with Marissa's other friend Dani. Both in their lilac dresses. Dani had her arm around Olivia's waist, as if she needed the support.

"The feathers," Olivia said. "Coming out of that guy's mouth. And then the squirrels . . ." Her voice faded out as she passed.

"Harmony, are you okay?"

I turned to see Uncle Kenny beside me. Max gave me a playful shove and ran off. Did the kid really expect me to play tag with him?

"Anything I can do?" Kenny asked.

I shook my head. "Thanks, Uncle Kenny. But—"

"Your parents must be frantic," he said.

I was touched that he was being so sympathetic and kind. But then he added, "Not to mention the expense. This must have set your dad back at least thirty thousand big ones. And all for nothing." He shook his head and did a tsk-tsk.

Uncle Kenny never changes.

"Let me know if there's anything I can do," he said.

Then he hurried after Max, who had decided to roll in the tall grass, despite the problem of getting grass stains on his wedding tuxedo.

He's a devil, I thought. *But a lovable one.*

And then a shadow rolled over me, and there stood Grandpa Bud. Standing a little too close, the way he always does. Wiping sweat off his forehead with one hand. His eyes locked on mine.

"Grandpa Bud—" I started.

But he brought his face up close to mine, so close our noses were almost touching. And he stared hard, as if peering into my soul, trying to penetrate my brain.

"Harmony—*what did you do?*"

TWENTY-SIX

"N-no," I stammered. I stumbled back. I lowered my gaze. His stare was *burning* me. "No, I didn't, Grandpa Bud. I didn't do anything."

He didn't move. He shielded his eyes from the sun with one hand and continued to lock his gaze on me. "Harmony—"

"I swear," I insisted. "Yes, I did those tricks last night. But I never—would never do anything to stop Marissa's wedding."

He still didn't move.

"I'm telling the truth," I said. "I had nothing to do with this, Grandpa. I . . . I don't know what happened to Marissa. But . . . we're all very frightened."

For the first time, I could feel the tears welling in my eyes. My throat tightened. I had to force back the sobs that threatened to erupt.

Grandpa Bud seemed satisfied. He took a step back, too. "Walk with me to the lodge?"

I took his arm. We started to walk. The tears felt hot on my cheeks. I held my breath to keep from crying.

He patted my hand. "Marissa will be okay," he said. "She's a Fear. Like you and me. We're not easy people, but we're resilient."

I didn't know how to respond to that. I walked my grandfather to the lodge. Everyone seemed to be gathering in the dining hall. I could see that the staff had begun to serve lunch.

That food was for the reception, I thought. And more tears began to slide down my face.

I wiped them off before I entered my parents' room. Mom was still in the armchair beside the couch. She had let her hair down and had a glass of brown liquid raised in one hand, probably scotch.

Robby sat hunched in a stiff-backed chair by the coffee table. He had his phone in his hands, but he wasn't using it. He kept his head down and didn't even look up when I walked in.

Dad and Doug stood behind the couch. They seemed to be in the middle of a heated discussion. Dad was gesturing with both hands. Doug had removed his tux's bow tie, and his shirt was open.

"Can you deny it?" Dad boomed. "Can you look me in the eye and tell me something wasn't going on between you two when you arrived?" His voice cracked on the last word. He swatted a fly off one cheek.

Doug shrugged his broad shoulders. He looked like he was ready to burst out of his tux, just explode from it. "What do you want me to say?"

Mom took a long sip of her drink. I stepped up beside her chair and squeezed her hand.

Dad hesitated. "I . . . I just want you to tell us if you know anything. If you can help explain—"

"Look," Doug said. "We weren't getting along, okay? But it was no big deal. Marissa always doubted everything. She was always thinking and rethinking. You know."

Dad nodded but didn't reply.

"So she said she was having second thoughts," Doug continued.

"And you didn't feel you should tell us?" Dad's voice rose to a shrill high note.

Doug shook his head. "Everyone knows that brides get the jitters. Maybe have their doubts. But . . . they always go through with the wedding." He swallowed and lowered his gaze.

Dad shook his head. He opened his mouth to say something but stopped. He wiped a tear from one eye.

And for the first time since Marissa disappeared, I thought of that wedding at this lodge all those years ago, and the sisters who went over the cliff.

This is a cursed place, Grandpa Bud had said.

No. No way. Marissa did not go over the cliff. Marissa drove away. Or walked. Or flew. But Marissa did not go over the cliff.

Dad gripped the back of the couch with both hands. "Doug, are you sure you didn't say something to Marissa to make her run away?"

Doug rolled his eyes. "Of course not. I told her I loved her. I told her I'd do everything to make sure our marriage worked. I made her believe me. I did."

Dad made a choking sound. "If you made her believe you, why is she gone?"

Doug shut his eyes. "I can't answer that. She . . . she was talking about our honeymoon. . . . You know. Our trip this fall. She . . . seemed really excited about it. I thought . . . I thought . . ."

His voice caught in his throat. He covered his face with both hands. His shoulders heaved up and down. I could tell he was crying.

Dad stepped forward and patted Doug on the shoulder. He turned to me with a helpless expression on his face. Dad isn't good around people who are crying.

Mom raised her glass, and he hurried to the bar to fill it. "We called the local police," she said to me. "They should be here soon."

And something about those words made me remember the note.

How could I have forgotten it all this time?

I guess all the emotion, all the shock and tension just froze my brain. I had stuffed it into the little bag I planned to carry at the wedding. I pulled it out and unfolded it.

"Look," I said. "I'm sorry. I found this. I meant to show it to you."

Doug had dropped onto the couch. He still had his head in his hands. He didn't move, but Dad and Robby walked over to me.

I held up the envelope. "I . . . I found this on the floor in Marissa's room as I was leaving."

Dad took it from me. He and Robby studied my scribbled name on the back, in red ballpoint ink. Dad's hand trembled as he pulled out the note, also in red ink.

DON'T LOOK FOR ME

"That's not Marissa's handwriting," Dad said. He squinted at it, brought it closer to his face. I could see his eyes move as he read the words again and again.

"Whoa. Wait a minute," Robby said. He took the note from Dad's hand. "Weird."

"What's weird?" I asked.

Robby studied it. "Nikki always writes in red ballpoint. It's sort of her thing. And the writing . . . Sometimes she prints like that."

"So?" I shook my head. "Nikki writes in red ink? So what? It couldn't be Nikki. Nikki isn't here, remember? And why would Nikki write a note for Marissa and address it to me?"

"Good question," Robby said. He handed the note back to me. "I'm just saying."

Dad rubbed his chin. "Save it for the police," he told me. "I guess it's too late for fingerprints. We've all handled it."

I was watching Robby. He was thinking so hard, I swear his face was turning red with the effort.

I poked him. "You don't think that Nikki—"

"No. But let's find out." He raised the phone. "I'll call her. It's crazy. But I just want to call and make sure."

He punched in the number. "I'll put it on speaker," he said.

The number started to ring.

We all froze in place. Mom set down her drink. Doug raised his head and watched.

The phone rang again. Again.

Four rings. Five. Six rings.

Robby lowered the phone. "She isn't answering," he murmured.

The phone rang one more time. Then we heard a click. And Nikki's voice: "Hey."

"Nikki?" Robby raised the phone. "Where are you?"

TWENTY-SEVEN

"Huh? I'm home," she said. "How was the wedding? Was it perfect? How did Marissa look?"

Robby hesitated. "Well . . . there wasn't a wedding, Nikki. It didn't happen."

"Are you joking? You're not serious."

"I'm serious," Robby said. "Marissa left. She . . . disappeared."

"Ohmigod," we heard Nikki cry. "Ohmigod. That's *horrible*." A long silence. "Robby, is everyone okay?"

"We're trying to deal with it," Robby said. "I think we're all in shock."

"Ohmigod," Nikki repeated. "I don't believe it. She just *left*? She didn't tell anyone?"

"We don't know what to think," Robby said. "Dad called the police. But we don't have a clue."

"How horrible."

"Listen, Nikki, are you really at home?"

"Of *course* I'm at home," she snapped. "Why do you keep asking me that question? Actually, my mom is calling me now. From the kitchen. I'd better go. But call me when you know anything, okay? Call me when you find her."

"Okay, I will," Robby said. But Nikki had already clicked off.

Robby pocketed the phone and turned to Dad. "You heard. She's at home."

Dad raised the envelope with the note inside. "Where are the police?" he said. "I have to show this to them."

And as he said that, two words flashed into my head. *Aiden Murray.*

It was like my brain had been put in a deep freeze. Only one thought thawed at a time. I should have remembered Aiden immediately.

What was wrong with me?

I realized I wasn't thinking clearly because I was more upset than I was allowing myself to show. Marissa and I aren't the closest sisters in the world, but I care about her.

I love her. And her disappearing without a trace, without a word, was too upsetting for me to deal with.

But now I was thinking clearly. Aiden Murray.

He acted so weird last night. So mysterious and cold. He had to have something to do with Marissa's disappearance.

Aiden was not invited. He had no business being here—except to cause trouble.

I started to the door. "Harmony, where are you going?" Mom called. Her voice sounded deeper, and she spoke slowly. The whiskey was having its effect.

"I'll be back in a few minutes," I said. "I—I have to find someone."

I opened the door and bumped into Uncle Kenny.

"Hey," he murmured. Then he edged past me. "Anything I can do?" he asked my parents. "Anyone you want me to call? Can I bring you some food?"

I didn't wait to hear their answers. I closed the door behind me, and turned down the hall. One more turn and a short stairway led me to the 200 row of rooms.

My conversation last night with Aiden ran through my mind as I strode toward room 237. It was not a friendly conversation.

This time I wouldn't let him get away with that. This time I would demand answers.

I took a deep breath and pounded hard on the door to his room. "Aiden, it's me," I shouted. "Open up. I need to talk to you."

I heard muffled voices from inside the room.

"Aiden? I know you can hear me," I shouted. "Open up, okay?"

The door swung open, and I stared at a man in a shiny blue suit. His hair was parted in the middle and slicked down against his head. He squinted at me with watery brown eyes through thick eyeglasses. "Hello. Can I help you?"

Behind him, I could see a dark-haired woman in a long brown dress watching us.

"I—I thought someone else was in here," I stammered. "I'm really sorry to bother you."

"No bother," the man said. He started to close the door.

"Did you just check in this morning?" I asked.

He narrowed his eyes at me. "No. Doris and I have been here for nearly a week. Since last Monday, actually."

"In this room?" I demanded.

"Yes. In this room." He smiled. "Hope you find who you're looking for." He closed the door.

I checked the number again. It was stenciled on the front of the door. Room 237. Definitely the room Aiden was in last night. I knew I had it right. I have a really good memory for numbers. And I remembered the round stain on the hall carpet to the right of the door.

But why would the man lie to me? He seemed like a nice guy.

Okay. Okay. There were more ways to figure this out.

Was Aiden's car still in the lot?

I pictured him climbing out of the car. The black hat tilted over his head. Pictured him striding up to the parking valet.

Yes. The valet. Tall with the red hair. I talked with him after he gave Aiden the ticket for his car. I remembered his name. Walter.

I grabbed the banister and half climbed, half slid down the stairs. Then I trotted to the front lobby. It was crowded with people. Some of them were our wedding guests, who seemed to be wandering around, unsure of what they should do.

I saw six unhappy-looking people carrying keyboards and guitars. The band we had hired. Leaving without performing. I knew Dad would have to pay them anyway. But they definitely looked disappointed.

Most of the guests were in the dining hall, having all the food that Marissa and Doug took weeks to select and taste. My stomach growled. I realized I hadn't had a bite since breakfast.

A couple of my cousins waved me over. I waved back but I kept going. I was on a mission. I had a strong feeling that if I solved the mystery of why Aiden was here, I'd know how we could find Marissa.

I pushed through the double doors of the entrance, nearly colliding with a baggage cart being pushed into the lodge by a white-uniformed valet. He had reddish hair, but he wasn't the guy I talked to last night.

I crossed the driveway, making my way toward the parking lot. The cars gleamed under the bright sunlight. The sun was still high above, the sky still cloudless. Perfect day for a wedding. Sigh.

No sign of Aiden's car.

I saw two attendants leaning against a wall at the valet stand. One of them was an older guy, gray hair under a blue baseball cap, slapping a rolled-up magazine against the leg of his uniform pants. The other appeared to be a teenager, tall and wiry, dark blue sunglasses over his eyes, hair shaved close to his head.

They turned as I ran up to them. "Did a guy in a red sports car leave this morning?" I asked breathlessly.

They exchanged glances. "Red sports car?" the older

one said. "I didn't see one."

"I just came on," his partner said. He ran his eyes over the board in front of him. It had all the car keys hanging on it, all of them labeled with ticket stubs.

"Is it still here?" I demanded.

The older guy scratched his head. "I haven't seen a red sports car. Do you know what make it is?"

I shook my head. "No. But I saw it here last night. I talked to the valet and—"

"You talked to Tony?" the teenager interrupted.

"No. I think his name was Walter," I said. I raised my hand above my head. "A really tall guy. Kind of a baby face. With wavy red hair?"

They exchanged glances again.

"Nope," the old guy said, shaking his head. "There's no Walter. Tony is short and bald. He walks with a little limp."

"No. I know I talked to a tall red-haired guy," I insisted. "He took the keys from my friend and gave him a valet ticket."

The old guy chuckled. "If he did, the guy is a car thief. Probably drove off with it."

My mouth dropped open. "Because—?"

"There's no tall red-haired valet who works here,"

the teenager said. He picked up some keys and rattled them, just to make some noise, I guess.

"Maybe talk to the manager. He might have hired on extra help. There's a big wedding here this weekend."

"Okay. The manager," I said. I turned and started back to the lodge entrance. I had to fight off a wave of dizziness.

That couple in the room where I knew Aiden had stayed. . . . These two guys claiming there was no tall, redheaded valet. Was I losing my mind? Something was messed up, and it was making me dizzy, making me feel as if I'd stepped into a *Twilight Zone* episode.

A young woman with short, straight blond hair and wearing bright red lipstick stood behind the front desk. I waited for a couple asking her if she had a map of the area. She pointed them to the concierge desk across the lobby.

Then I stepped up to the counter. The name on the badge on her jacket lapel read: *Lisa*. She typed something on her computer, then raised her eyes to me with a smile. "Can I help you?"

"I need to see the manager," I said.

Her smile faded. "Is there a problem?"

I didn't know how to answer that. "Actually, there are a *lot* of problems," I said. "But I just want to ask for some information about a guest."

She nodded. For some reason, she kept her fingers on the computer keyboard. "Well, I'm the Sunday manager," she said. "My boss doesn't come in on weekends."

"Well, can you help me, Lisa?" I asked. "I'm with the wedding party. Last night, I spoke to a guest here named Aiden Murray. I just want to know if he checked out. You're allowed to tell me that, right?"

She blinked. I think my intensity surprised her. "Yes, I can help you with that," she said. She lowered her eyes to the screen and typed for a long while.

Then she frowned. "You said the name was Aiden? Can you spell the last name for me?"

I spelled it. She typed some more. "Hmmm. It's not coming up." She typed some more. "Are you sure he checked in under his own name?"

"I know I talked with him. He was in room 237."

She nodded. "Room 237." She typed, then squinted at the screen. "No, that's not the right room, I'm afraid. We've had a couple staying in there since Monday. His name isn't Slocum, is it?"

I gritted my teeth. "Aiden Murray. Murray."

She brushed a hand through her short hair. She let out a long breath. "Must be some mix-up. I'm so sorry.

That name just doesn't come up on my computer. Aiden Murray has never been a guest at this lodge."

I had the urge to pound my fists on the computer top, but I controlled myself. "This is crazy," I murmured. "I was at this desk last night. I saw Aiden's name on the screen."

Lisa narrowed her eyes at me. "You saw this screen?"

I nodded. "The guy, Mr. Himuro, he stepped away for a moment to answer a call, and I read the screen while he was away. You know. Just to find Aiden's room number."

Lisa pressed a hand on her forehead. "I'm sorry. You're confusing me. Who did you say stepped away from the desk?"

"Mr. Himuro," I said. "He told me Aiden was here, but he wasn't allowed to tell me—"

"The night manager is Phillip Brandt," Lisa interrupted. "Blond guy, stubble of beard on his face, looks a little like Ryan Gosling?"

"No. Mr. Himuro," I insisted.

"This is very weird." She stared at me, as if trying to read my mind, see if I was some kind of nutjob. "The lodge doesn't have anyone working here named Mr. Himuro."

"But—" I gripped the countertop. The dizziness

swept back, making the room tilt in front of me.

No redheaded valet? No Mr. Himuro? No red sports car? No Aiden in room 237?

But they were all real last night, and I knew I wasn't dreaming now.

"I'm so sorry I couldn't help you," Lisa said. She was still studying me. "I really can't explain the confusion."

"Neither can I," I murmured. I didn't want to let go of the counter. I felt that my knees would collapse and I would form a puddle on the floor, just melt away and disappear like Mr. Himuro and the valet last night.

Lisa lowered her eyes to her keyboard and began to type. I knew she was just waiting for me to leave.

I let out a long sigh, let go of the countertop, and started to back away. But something on the wall caught my eye.

The wall to the left of the reception desk was covered with framed black-and-white photos, old photos of groups of people. They were all standing out in front of the lodge, all in lodge uniforms, all smiling.

"Lisa, I'm sorry," I said, my eyes on one of the old photos. "Could I see that photo?"

She stood up, her face knotted in confusion. "A photo? I don't understand."

"That one," I said, pointing. "The third one from the top." I knew I sounded frantic, like a crazy person. But the face in the photo . . .

Lisa stood on tiptoes to reach the framed photograph. She gripped it in both hands and raised it off its hook. Then she carried it over and set it down in front of me on the counter.

"These are old photographs taken over the years of the workers at this lodge," she said. "I think my grandmother is in one of them."

I could barely hear her words. I was squinting hard at a face in the front row of this old photo. I grabbed the frame by its sides and brought it close to my face.

"That's *him*!" I shrieked. I stabbed the glass over the face with my finger. "See?" I turned it so Lisa could see.

She followed my pointer finger. "That's *who*?"

"Mr. Himuro," I said. "That's the man I talked to here last night."

Lisa gazed at it for a long moment. Then she raised her eyes to me. "But—"

"And look!" I cried. "That guy in the back row. On the end? See him? That's the parking valet from last night. I'm sure it is. Tall and red-haired. I mean, it's black and white. But you can see his hair is light. That's him!"

She took the photograph from me and studied it for a moment. Then she turned it over. "There's a date on the back," she said.

"Huh? What does it say?" I demanded.

She squinted at the little rectangular label on the back of the frame. "I—I'm so sorry," she stammered. "You must be mistaken. It says this photo is from 1924."

TWENTY-EIGHT

I had to force myself to breathe. My head suddenly felt light, as if it could float away. The voices in the lobby faded from my ears, and all I could hear were my own racing heartbeats.

Himuro and the valet. That was them. Definitely them. In the photo—from 1924. I knew I had talked to them.

But of course it was totally impossible.

"Thank you," I managed to say. I spun away from the reception desk and took a few unsteady steps across the lobby. My cousins were still sitting at a table near the back wall. They waved to me again, but I pretended I didn't see them.

I have to get back to my parents, I thought. *They must wonder where I've been all this time.*

Could I tell them? Could I tell them the truth? Tell them I'd lost my mind? That I'd been seeing people from over ninety years ago?

No, I decided. *If I tell them, it will only add to the confusion, add to everyone's unhappiness.* I wanted to shut myself in my room and just think. Try to figure this out. Try to make sense of this insane thing that happened to me.

This is a cursed place. Grandpa Bud's words came back to me again. He knew the whole story of the Fear family wedding from 1924. But did he know more? Did he know more about this lodge and the curse than he had told me?

Maybe Grandpa Bud could help me make sense of it. Help convince me that I wasn't going totally insane.

Then I thought: *He is an old man. He's frail. He must be seriously upset about Marissa's disappearance.* Would it be fair to add to his burden?

I didn't know what to do. I only knew I had to get back to my family and see if there was any news about my sister.

So I made my way across the crowded, noisy lobby,

trying to shut out everyone, shut out the voices, shut out the spinning thoughts inside my head.

And there he was in front of me.

"Ohmigod!" I uttered. I nearly tripped over my own shoes. There was Aiden walking toward the bar.

He had his back turned. He was only a few steps in front of me. I recognized the little black hat first, and then his blond hair sticking out over the back of his neck.

He wore a trench coat, and its belt was unfastened and trailed along the floor. He was taking long strides, and I had to run to catch up to him.

Breathing hard, I stepped up behind him and touched him on the shoulder.

He spun around—and I let out a startled cry.

TWENTY-NINE

"Hello," he said. "Can I help you?"

I stared into his face. It wasn't Aiden.

He was older, in his thirties maybe, with circles around his dark eyes, cheeks sagging, tired-looking, a weary face. Salt-and-pepper mustache and a few days' stubble.

Not Aiden's face.

Was this who I saw last night?

No. Of course not. I spoke to Aiden. In room 237. We spoke. He knew my name. It wasn't this man. This imposter. This man in the black hat with Aiden's walk.

"I . . . I'm sorry," I choked out. "I thought you were someone else."

"No worries," he said. "Have a good one." He turned and strode away.

When I returned to my parents' room, it looked as if no one had moved. Mom was still in the armchair, drink in one hand, a bunched-up handkerchief gripped in the other. Dad stood behind her chair, looking pale and unsteady. Robby sat at the table behind them, rolling his phone between his fingers.

Doug stood beside the table, phone to his ear. He lowered it as I entered the room. "I keep calling her," he said, "but it goes right to voice mail." He sighed. "She doesn't answer my texts, either. It says they are delivered, but she doesn't reply."

Silence. We stared at each other.

"Where've you been, Harmony?" Dad asked finally.

"I had a few ideas," I said. "But they . . . they were a waste of time."

Mom shook her head. "I—I don't know what to think. I can't believe Marissa would be this inconsiderate. It just isn't like her. She would have called. She . . . she must be in trouble." She swallowed and made a coughing sound. "Oh my God. She could be . . . dead."

"Don't *say* that!" Dad shouted. "Why do you always have to go to the worst possible thing? Marissa isn't dead.

I know she isn't. Try to be more positive."

Mom sipped her drink. "Positive? My daughter is missing on her wedding day, and I'm supposed to be positive?"

A knock on the door interrupted the conversation.

"Who is it?" Dad shouted.

"Kenny."

Dad frowned. "I know what *he* wants. The police won't let anyone go home until they've all been questioned."

The door swung open and Uncle Kenny strode in, followed by Max, who carried a red plastic fire truck. Max dropped instantly to the rug and began pushing his fire truck around, making annoying siren noises.

Kenny had changed from his wedding suit into a loose-fitting blue polo shirt and khaki shorts. "Sorry to barge in again," he said. "But they won't let me check out, and I have an important meeting that just came up this minute in Philly tomorrow."

"Kenny, how about a drink?" Mom said, raising her glass to him. She was beginning to slur her words, and her voice was throaty, kind of deep and fuzzy.

Kenny shook his bald head impatiently. "I'm going to miss my plane unless the cops let me out of here. Do you think you could talk to them, David?"

"I could try," Dad said reluctantly. I could see the anger in his eyes. Even in an emergency like this one, Kenny had to be a pain.

Max sent his fire truck smashing into the wall. He laughed and retrieved it and made more siren wails. You'd think maybe he'd notice the sadness in the room, but he didn't.

Lucky kid.

Meanwhile, I still felt dazed by my encounter in the lobby, and not just with the guy who looked like Aiden. I kept seeing that old photograph from 1924, kept seeing the two guys I talked to posing in there so long ago.

I'm crazy. Marissa's disappearance has totally knocked my brain off balance.

Dad stepped away from the chair and started toward the door. "If I can find the police, Kenny, maybe I can ask them to interview you first."

"I don't think there's time. It's an hour drive to the airport. Can't you just tell them I'm your brother and there's no reason—"

"I saw Marissa." Max's words made everyone freeze.

He sat with his legs crossed, spinning the fire truck wheel against his palm.

"What did you say?" I asked.

"I saw Marissa," he repeated.

"When?"

"This morning." He lowered the truck to the rug and sent it rolling toward the wall.

Mom climbed to her feet, spilling some of her drink. "Where, Max? Where did you see her?"

No one moved. We all stared down at him, cross-legged and nonchalant on the floor.

"In the lobby," Max replied, standing up. "Before the wedding. Want me to show you?"

"Yes. Show us." Uncle Kenny placed his hands on Max's shoulders. He turned back to my dad. "But quickly, because we really have to leave. I don't mean to be difficult, but if I miss this meeting . . ."

Dad held the door open. "We don't all have to go," he said, motioning to Mom. "Why don't you stay, and I'll report back right away."

Mom settled back into the chair.

"I'll stay with Mom," Robby said.

Doug followed Dad and me to the door. "Where are we going?" Kenny asked Max.

Max gripped the fire truck in one hand. He pointed with his other hand. "To the lobby. Can I have an ice cream?"

"Not right now," Kenny said.

"But I want one," Max insisted.

We turned the corner. The lobby was at the end of this hallway.

"You're sure you saw Marissa?" Dad asked Max, stepping up beside him. "This morning? You're sure?"

Max nodded. "Yes. I saw her."

"Did she talk to you?" Doug asked.

"Of course not," Max said. "That's dumb."

Doug and I exchanged glances again. Max's answer made no sense.

We stepped into the lobby. The crowd had thinned out. A family of four was checking in at the front desk. The seats where I'd seen my cousins were empty.

"Max, show us where you saw Marissa," Kenny said. He'd been holding on to Max's shoulders the whole way. Now he let go of them.

"Over here," Max said. He took off, running toward the front doors. He stopped at the steps that led down to the exit. He turned toward an easel propped up at the side.

"Here she is. Right here," Max proclaimed.

I gasped. He was pointing at the sign announcing the wedding. It was a large photo of Marissa and Doug, and it had words in a fancy script beneath it: *The Wedding of*

Marissa Fear and Douglas Falkner. 1 p.m. On the Mesa Today.

Max stabbed the photo with his finger. "See? I *told* you I saw her. Can I have ice cream? I want vanilla."

They looked so happy in the photo, big smiles and their arms around each other. I had to force back a sob. Dad just shook his head, his eyes shut. For once, Uncle Kenny was speechless.

Doug, still in his tuxedo, but the tie gone and the shirt open a few buttons at the collar, one side untucked, shoved his hands into his pockets. He had his head down. I couldn't see his expression.

"Ice cream!" Max shouted.

Kenny turned to Dad and shrugged. "Sorry about that." He started leading the kid away. "Better find him some ice cream. David, you'll get me out of here, right?"

Dad didn't answer. We turned and started to walk back to the room.

But a shout from the entrance doors made us stop. "Mr. Fear, can I see you for a moment?"

The three of us spun around to see a blond-haired, very young policeman come up the stairs. He had a badge pinned to his blue short-sleeved uniform shirt. His black gun holster bounced against his leg as he hurried toward us.

"I have to ask you a question," he said, a little out of breath. His eyes were olive-colored, and he had a spray of freckles around his nose.

He raised a blue-and-red running shoe in front of him. "Do you recognize this?" he asked.

We all squinted at it as if we'd never seen a sneaker before.

"Is it your daughter's?" the officer asked, pushing it closer to us.

"Could be. I can't tell," Dad said softly.

"Where did you find it?" I asked.

"On the mesa. At the edge of the cliff."

THIRTY

Dad grabbed my arm. "Do you recognize it? Is it Marissa's?"

I squinted hard at it. "I don't recognize it. I'm sorry. I can't remember seeing her wear it. But I don't know."

The officer lowered the shoe to his side. "We called the state police," he said. "They have choppers that can fly over the canyon and search the canyon floor."

Dad gasped and gripped my arm harder. "You mean—"

"Looking for her body?" Doug said, his voice just above a whisper.

"There's probably no one down there," the policeman replied. His olive eyes locked on Doug. "A shoe doesn't mean anything. But we have to look."

I covered my face with my hands. My knees suddenly felt weak. I held on to Dad.

"We think she left early this morning," Dad said. "Maybe before breakfast." His eyes questioned the young officer.

"We had a long talk with the parking valet on duty this morning, sir. He didn't see anyone with your daughter's description leave on her own."

"Did he mention a blond man in a red sports car?" I asked. Once again, I pictured Aiden being handed a ticket by the tall red-haired valet I had spoken to.

The officer scratched his head. "No. He didn't. Should I ask him about that? Do you think Miss Fear might have left with this man?"

Dad and Doug were staring at me.

"You can ask," I said. "But I'm pretty sure he'll say no."

We walked back to my parents' room in silence, each with our own frightening thoughts. Dad stopped outside the door. "Harmony, what was that about a guy in a sports car?"

"Not worth mentioning," I said, knowing that I was lying. But I was still way too confused to talk about it. "We can talk about it later, Dad. It's not important."

He studied me for a long moment, then pushed open the door.

While we were away, Grandpa Bud had showed up. He had pulled an armchair across from Mom, and the two of them had drinks in their hands. He had changed into a baggy gray sweatshirt and faded jeans.

Robby was stretched out on the couch, eyes shut and mouth open, sound asleep. My brother can sleep through anything. I guess it's one way to deal with the worst family tragedy imaginable.

"Well?" Mom demanded, a teardrop running down one cheek.

"A wild-goose chase," I told her. "Max took us to see the photo of Marissa on the wedding poster in the lobby."

Mom sank in her chair. The glass tilted in her hand but didn't spill.

Dad had his hands clasped tightly in front of him. "The police found a running shoe," he said. "We didn't recognize it. They found it at the edge of the cliff." He just blurted it all out in one breath.

Mom and Grandpa Bud both gasped. On the couch, Robby stirred and shifted onto his side but didn't wake up.

"At the cliff? Do they—do they think it's Marissa's?" Mom stammered.

Dad shook his head. "They don't know. They've got helicopters searching the canyon floor."

"Oh no," Mom moaned. "Oh no. Oh no." She buried her head in her hands.

Grandpa Bud reached out to comfort her. "We can't assume the worst," he said.

Doug was punching his phone again. "Marissa wouldn't kill herself," he said. "Maybe she decided she didn't want to marry me. But I know she'd never kill herself. That's just crazy."

He listened to his phone. "Just voice mail again." He tossed the phone angrily onto the table. "She didn't kill herself," he repeated through gritted teeth. "Trust me. I know her."

"Doug is right—" I started.

But Doug wasn't finished. "Marissa just panicked and left. I don't care what the parking valet says. I know I'm right." He slammed a fist on the tabletop. "We had words. We had a big argument yesterday. I swear I don't even remember what it was about. And believe me, it wasn't anything for Marissa to kill herself over. So let's just stop thinking that way."

He was red-faced now and shaking.

"Sit down, Doug," Dad said. "We know you have to be right. But don't get yourself in a frenzy."

"A frenzy?" Doug repeated. But he followed Dad's instruction. He sat down in a chair beside the table.

Robby made a snorting sound but didn't wake up. How could he sleep through this whole discussion, through all the tension?

Grandpa Bud burped loudly. He set down his drink and covered his mouth with one hand. "Pardon me. My stomach is doing flip-flops. This is too much for an old man to bear."

"Do you want to lie down?" Dad asked.

Bud shook his head. "I won't be able to sleep. I'm too wired to take a nap, and too worried."

"Why hasn't she called?" Mom asked. I could see that her eyes weren't focusing. Mom was in her own world of shock and confusion.

"We all knew this was a cursed place," Grandpa Bud said. "We all knew about the wedding here in 1924. A member of the Goode family awoke the curse between the two families and—"

"Stop it, Bud!" Mom screamed. "*Stop* it. Do you really think talking about what happened nearly a hundred years ago is going to do any good today?"

She jumped unsteadily to her feet. "Let's talk about something else. Is it supposed to be sunny tomorrow? Has anyone seen the baseball scores? Try the TV. There should be a game on this afternoon. I'm sure we can find someone to root for."

Dad swept his arms around her and guided her back down into the chair. "Shhhhh. Shhhhh." He whispered some things to her that I couldn't hear.

Mom shut her eyes. Her shoulders were shaking, but she wasn't crying. Dad stood silently, a steady hand on her trembling shoulder.

The room grew quiet. We were all having our private thoughts. Sad thoughts. Of course, I had guilty thoughts. Now I felt total guilt for the pranks I had played. . . . The feathers in Uncle Kenny's mouth . . . the horror-movie stampede of the squirrels in the dark of night.

What was I *thinking*? Why did I think it would be hilarious to disrupt Marissa's wedding like that? Of course, I had no way of knowing that she would disappear into thin air.

But still . . .

If something terrible happened to Marissa, would I ever forgive myself? Had I doomed myself to a lifetime of guilt?

A knock on the door made us all sit up alert, even Robby. The blue-uniformed cop with the strange olive eyes stepped into the room.

His expression told it all. His face was set in a tight-lipped frown. His eyes swept the room once, then avoided us, his stare above our heads as if he couldn't bear the pain of looking at us.

"Bad news, I'm afraid," he said, just loud enough for us to hear. He cleared his throat. "Our chopper patrol—"

"NO!" Mom let out a scream and jumped up, knocking over her glass. Grandpa Bud made a grab for her, but she stumbled toward the officer, shaking her head, mouthing the word *no*.

The cop raised his eyes to Dad, who had frozen beside Mom's chair and didn't even seem to realize that Mom was stumbling across the room. "I'm sorry, folks," he said, and had to clear his throat again. "But the state police found a body at the bottom of the cliff. A girl's. I mean, a young woman's body."

"No no no no." Mom raised both fists as if she was about to attack the officer for bringing the news.

Dad finally moved. He took Mom's arms and held her back. Then he spread an arm around her shoulders. He pressed his forehead to her cheek and whispered again.

I glimpsed Grandpa Bud, leaning forward in his chair, very pale, his hand on his chest. I silently prayed the officer's news wasn't giving him a heart attack.

Robby sat upright on the couch, blinking hard, stunned from his nap, squinting at the young cop as if trying to decide if it was all part of a dream. Doug collapsed onto a chair at the table and covered his head in his hands.

My mind drifted away. I saw Marissa as a little girl, dressed up for Sunday school. A picture of her in her high school graduation robe flashed into my brain. A crazy jumble of pictures with no reason or pattern.

"We need someone to identify the body," the cop was saying. "One of you should come with us." And then he added, thoughtlessly, "The body is crushed but the face is pretty much untouched."

A detail we really didn't need. But I guessed we should cut him some slack. The officer looked green, about to vomit. He probably didn't get too many young girls hauled up from the cliff bottom.

Mom opened her mouth in a deafening animal wail and began to sob, her chest and shoulders heaving. Dad awkwardly reached for her, but she twisted out of his grasp and continued to wail.

"I'll go with you," Doug said to the officer. He started to stand up.

"They'd prefer it to be a family member," the cop said.

Doug made a gurgling sound and slumped back into his chair.

I could see that Dad had his hands full with Mom.

Robby was still fighting his way out of his daze. "I'll go," I said.

"No—" Dad started to protest. "It should be me."

Mom picked up her drink glass and heaved it at the wall.

After the shattering sound had stopped echoing through my head, I stepped forward. "I'll go, Dad. I'll be okay."

"Robby, snap out of it," Dad said. "Take care of your mother. We'll be right back."

Dad and I followed the cop out of the room.

I must have been in some kind of dream state. I kept seeing these pictures in my head of Marissa and me when we were little. Building clubhouses out of cardboard boxes. Marissa reading her chapter books to me before I knew how to read myself. My heart was fluttering in my chest. It felt like hummingbird wings. But I didn't feel the kind of cold dread you would expect.

Not until Dad and I followed the path up from the lodge and I saw the huddle of blue-uniformed officers at the top of the mesa. When I saw them, my breath escaped my body as if I had been punched in the stomach.

Dad must have seen my sudden terror. He gently took my arm and guided me through the tall grass to the circle of cops.

"Let us by," the cop said in a low voice, and the circle opened up.

I saw a green canvas tarp on the grass, and I could make out the shape of a body in the bulge at its center. "Oh." A single word escaped my mouth.

Dad squeezed my hand. I struggled to breathe. But the bird wings had risen from my chest into my mouth. And my legs now felt as if they each weighed five hundred pounds. I couldn't take another step.

Two officers bent and took the ends of the canvas tarp in their hands.

"We just need you both to take a quick look and identify her." I struggled to make sense of his words. They suddenly didn't seem to be in a language I understood.

I couldn't reply. I just stood there trembling, not breathing, not thinking, the sunlight suddenly blinding, pain pulsing at the sides of my head.

The two cops slowly pulled the tarp back, revealing the pale, pale face.

"NOOOO!" I couldn't stop the scream that burst from my throat. "NOOOOO! NOOOOOOOO!"

PART FOUR

THIRTY-ONE

My brain reeling, the sunlight pulsing in my eyes, I stared at the dead girl's face. Taylor. Taylor Mancuso. Marissa's maid of honor. Marissa's best friend.

Her blue eyes were open, glassy but lifeless. Gazing up at me as if trying to see me. Her mouth had a layer of coral lipstick, still fresh and smooth. Her lips were parted slightly and her tongue fell limply through her teeth.

She must have landed on the back of her head because her face seemed almost untouched. I could see that her skull was crushed, and her blond hair was caked with dark dried blood.

"It's . . . not." My father choked on the words.

"It's Taylor Mancuso," I cried out. "Not Marissa. It's not Marissa."

Dad wrapped his arms around me. I could feel him trembling. He tried to speak but no sound came out.

The officers slid the tarp back over her face. But I could still see her. Still see her glassy eyes . . . her open lips . . . her pretty face. Taylor's pretty face . . .

I heard her voice. I heard her laugh. I pictured Taylor and Marissa in our den, music thumping, dancing, practicing new dance moves. Laughing, always laughing. Taylor and Marissa, like twittering birds. Like . . . birds of a feather.

Crazy thoughts.

Dad gripped my shoulders. He still hadn't spoken.

"Can I help you back to the lodge?" The cop leaned into the dazzling sunlight, a shadow in front of my face.

I turned to him. "Do you have a name?" Why did that question burst out of me?

"Sergeant Grady," he said.

"Help us back, Sergeant."

He took my arm. Dad held on to my other arm. "I . . . I don't believe it." He finally found his voice.

"Was she pushed?" I asked.

Sergeant Grady pointed to the dirt at the cliff edge. "I really can't say. But there's no sign of a struggle."

We walked a few steps along the path to the lodge.

"Do you think someone had a reason to push her?" he asked, brushing a horsefly off my forehead.

"Of course not," I snapped.

"Just asking. We have to ask the questions, you know. How well did you know her?"

I shrugged. "She was Marissa's best friend."

"She wasn't depressed or anything, was she?" Grady turned his olive eyes on me, studying me. "She didn't act strange at the wedding rehearsal?"

"Taylor never acted strange," I said. My voice cracked. I hated thinking about her in the past tense. "She was totally normal, a good girl. You know?"

He nodded.

We walked on. He had a thoughtful look frozen on his face. "So . . . you're saying she wouldn't jump."

"No," I murmured.

Then I noticed the roar in my ears. I turned and saw a black helicopter rising over the side of the mesa. Dad squeezed my hand. He saw it, too.

"They're still looking?" I asked Grady.

He nodded. "Maybe your sister fell with her."

"Huh? Fell?"

"Maybe they were together. In the morning. Maybe they were kidding around. Before the wedding. And maybe one of them started to fall and the other one tried to save her and—"

I shuddered.

"Just trying to think of everything," he said, avoiding my stare. "The state guys have been in the air a long time now, and they haven't found anyone else down there. So maybe . . ."

"Maybe Marissa decided she didn't want to marry Doug, and she took off. Escaped. Early this morning," Dad said.

Grady nodded. "Better a missing person case than a homicide or an accident. We can't declare her missing until she's been gone for twenty-four hours. But you should check her credit cards and bank accounts. Look for any unusual charges or withdrawals."

Was I supposed to play detective now?

I couldn't. I wanted to shout and cry and scream and wail and throw myself on the grass and pound the dirt till my fists bled. I wanted the world to see how much I wanted my sister, and wanted her back now. But instead I kept walking between Dad and Grady.

We were nearly back at the lodge now. The roar of the helicopter over the mesa had faded to a distant hum in my ears. I crossed my fingers on both hands and silently prayed they wouldn't find Marissa sprawled and broken on the cliff bottom.

Sergeant Grady pulled open the entrance door for us. I pictured the scene in my parents' room. And I imagined the horror—and the relief—everyone in there was about to feel.

Dad stayed at the lodge. He said that someone had to stay in case the local police came up with anything. Robby and I took Mom and Grandpa Bud to the airport.

We put Bud on a flight back to Cincinnati. "Promise me . . . ," he started.

"I promise we'll call you as soon as we hear anything," I told him.

At the gate, he leaned close as if to kiss me good-bye. But instead, he whispered, "When you stir the pot, unexpected things emerge. No more tricks, Harmony. None."

"Of course not," I whispered back.

But he started me thinking. *Was there a spell to bring Marissa back? Was there some kind of magic in those old books in our attic to reveal to me where Marissa was?*

If she is dead, could I bring her back? Is the Fear magic that powerful? Am I?

Probably not.

Weird thoughts, for sure. But I couldn't control them.

And, actually, I didn't want to.

"Where's Douglas?" Mom asked as we waited at gate 12 to board our plane. Mom was still in a fog. She hadn't seemed at all relieved when I told her that it wasn't Marissa at the bottom of the canyon. It was as if her mind just couldn't bear all that had happened. She hadn't snapped or anything. It was just like she was half asleep. Her body was going through the motions, her mind still lingering in some kind of dream.

"Doug went on an earlier plane," Robby said.

Mom nodded. She folded her hands over the pocketbook in her lap.

Robby had his thumbs moving over the keyboard on his phone. I knew he had to be texting Nikki, telling her we were on our way back to Shadyside.

I had a gnawing hunger. Maybe because I hadn't eaten a real meal since Marissa disappeared before the wedding. I'd bought a giant Snickers bar at one of the airport stores, and I devoured the whole thing in ten seconds.

I could see that Robby was watching me. "Are you okay?"

"Not really," I said. What should I say? That I was just fine?

"Maybe Marissa will be home waiting for us when

we get there," Mom said. She had a strange, dreamy smile on her face.

"Maybe," Robby said, glancing at me.

"Mom," I said. "She hasn't called, and she doesn't answer her phone. If she is home . . ." My voice trailed off. I didn't know how to finish my sentence.

Mom nodded. She had a copy of *Food & Wine* magazine rolled up between her hands, but she made no attempt to look at it. Robby and I stared at our phones until it was time to board the plane.

"What's new with Nikki?" I asked, just to be saying something.

He shrugged. "Not much."

I had a short text conversation with my friend Sophie back in Shadyside. She was excited about some new shoe store at the mall. Sophie is a shoe freak, although she can't afford any of the shoes she likes.

I was desperate to tell her about what happened at the wedding and how Marissa had disappeared, but it just didn't seem like the kind of thing to spring on someone in a text message.

On the plane, Robby and I sat together. Mom was at the far end of the row. I couldn't hold it in any longer. I pushed Robby's phone away from his face, tugged his earbuds from his ears, and told him I had to talk to him.

He rolled his eyes. "Are you going to tell me some kind of conspiracy theory about the wedding?"

"It's not a theory," I said. "It's what happened to me. Shut up and listen. I saw Aiden Murray at the lodge."

That got my brother's attention.

I was so desperate to share the story with someone, I blurted it out in a breathless wave of words. I told Robby how I saw Aiden park his red sports car and go into the lodge. How I spoke with him at the door to his room but he wouldn't tell me why he was there.

"I know he has something to do with Marissa disappearing," I said. "I *know* he does."

Robby narrowed his eyes at me. "Harmony, are you kidding me? Why didn't you tell anyone about this before? Why didn't you tell Mom or Dad—or the police?"

I took a breath. "Because the story gets all mixed up," I said. "I tried to find Aiden after Marissa vanished, but he wasn't in his room. Another couple was in there, and they said they had been in the room for a week."

"You had the wrong room?" Robby asked.

"No. I had the *right* room," I insisted. "So I tried to track Aiden down with the desk clerk and the parking valet. But they weren't the same. They were different people. And they didn't know the men I had talked to."

I saw my brother's expression.

"I'm not making sense—*am I?*"

"Not much," he said.

"Well, it gets crazier," I said. I hesitated. I didn't want Robby to think I was crazy. But I had to tell him the insane, impossible part of the story.

"There was a photo on the wall behind the front desk," I said. "An old photo of the lodge workers, from 1924. And . . . And I swear, Robby, the desk clerk and the parking guy I talked to—they were in that old photo."

Robby nodded. His expression didn't show any surprise. His eyes locked on mine.

I waited for him to react. To say something. Anything. But he didn't move a muscle.

A cold feeling tightened the back of my neck. "Do you believe me?" I asked, gripping his arm. "Please say you believe me."

"Did you see *me* in the photo?" he said finally. His face was slack and his eyes bored into mine. "I was the bellhop in the long red coat and bow tie."

THIRTY-TWO

I let out a growl and punched his shoulder. "Not funny. Come on, I'm serious. I'm trying to tell you—"

He pushed my hand away. "You know, the lodge is six thousand feet up. Sometimes a high altitude can mess with the oxygen to your brain."

I wanted to kill him. I tried to confide in him, to tell him a truly frightening thing that had happened to me. And he had to act like I was crazy or overcome with altitude sickness.

"Look, Robby—" I started.

The plane hit a bump. I grabbed the bottle of water I had on the tray in front of me.

"Were you telling me about a *Twilight Zone* episode you saw?" Robby said. "You can't really expect me—"

"Yes, I did," I snapped. "I expected you to listen to me and believe me and help me figure out what happened."

I didn't realize I was shouting until I saw two people turn around to stare at me. Down the row, Mom didn't lift her head from the magazine she had finally opened.

Robby tapped his fingers on the chair arm. The plane bumped again. "Okay. Let's see. You saw Aiden, even though he vanished last year and had no business being at the wedding. And then you talked to some hotel workers from 1924. Did I get that right?"

"Look. I know it sounds insane. There's got to be an explanation, right?"

He didn't reply. He gazed out the window. The sky was a solid blue, bright and clear. "Say something," I insisted.

"I don't know what to say, Harmony. I'm just thinking about those weird jokes you played. Those spells you cast." He raised his eyes to mine. "The fact that you . . . you're a *witch*."

I uttered a short cry. "I am *not*, idiot. I'm not a witch. I'm a Fear."

"And that means exactly what?"

"I taught myself how to do that stuff from books in our attic," I told him. "You could do it, too."

He shook his head. "No way. I don't want to get into

that kind of stuff. Maybe you *are* crazy."

He turned in his seat to face me. "You know why you did those things at the wedding, Harmony?" he said. "Because you're so jealous of Marissa. Don't deny it. You know you've always been jealous of her."

"Robby—"

"In your twisted mind, you just wanted to win something. You wanted to show Marissa. Show her who had the power, I guess."

"You're insane," I said.

"No, I'm not. And I'd never hurt Marissa. I'd never cast spells like those. I'd never try to spoil her big day like that. And I'd never stir up whatever"—his voice dropped to a whisper—"whatever evil our ancestors were up to back in the day. Because that's what it is. Evil. Maybe that's why you're drawn to it."

Robby's words really stung. I felt a throbbing pain in my chest, and I felt like I was going to burst out sobbing.

"That's totally unfair!" I cried, again loud enough to make people turn around. "I played some mean tricks. I shouldn't have done it. But I would never hurt Marissa. You . . . you don't suspect me, do you? You don't think I made her disappear?"

Robby's expression was hard and cold. "I don't know what to think."

I could see that I'd made a terrible mistake. What made me think that I could confide in Robby? Even though he was my twin, he was on Marissa's side in just about every argument. Even when we were little kids.

Well, none of that mattered now.

Marissa was gone. Our family was broken. Most likely, what lay ahead for us now were tears and horror and years of sadness.

Up till that moment, I'd forced myself to stay optimistic about finding Marissa. But now, sitting silently beside Robby, the two of us avoiding each other's eyes, I gave in to the darkness, gave in to the idea that our lives were ruined forever.

And then, when we landed in Shadyside and the taxi pulled up to our driveway, the darkness lifted in an instant.

"The car!" Mom cried.

Yes, Marissa's blue Fusion stood halfway up the driveway.

"It's here!" Mom scrambled out of the taxi, nearly falling on her face in her rush to the house. Robby scurried around to her side to help her gain her balance.

My heart jumped into my throat. But only for a second. And then I sighed. "Wait. Her car was *always* here," I reminded them, my voice breaking. "She didn't take her car, remember?"

A groan escaped Mom's throat. Her whole body slumped. Robby held her up.

I hoisted the suitcases from the trunk of the taxi. The driver helped me carry them to the front walk. I paid him and watched him walk back to his car. Mom and Robby were still halfway up the driveway.

"Oh." I murmured my surprise when I saw someone move in the front window. Sunlight reflected off the window glass. The room was dark behind it.

But I saw someone move. Saw a face, just for an instant. A shoulder. A flash of white. Yes. A white top. And someone walking quickly, caught for a second in the golden glare of the window.

I tore up the front stoop. Fumbled in my bag for the key. Tugged the door open wide and leaped into the entryway.

"Marissa?" I shouted. "Marissa? Where *are* you?"

THIRTY-THREE

Mom and Robby crowded behind me. It was warm inside the house, and the living room smelled of floor polish or some kind of cleaner.

"Marissa?"

I heard the rapid tap of footsteps in the back hall. My heart tapped along with each beat. I strode forward, eager to see her, to throw my arms around her, to feel her warm cheek against mine.

I stopped when the blond woman in the white top came into view. "Ada?" Her name burst from my mouth, high and shrill. "Ada?"

She smiled. "You're home early. How was the wedding?"

Mom and Robby gazed at her in silence.

Ada Barnes. Our tall, beautiful housekeeper who should be a supermodel. I hadn't remembered that she'd be working today.

Her smile faded. She brushed a hand through her short, wavy hair. "You all look exhausted. Is everything okay?"

"Not really," I said. I didn't want to tell her the whole story. My head was spinning. Pain throbbed at my temples. The hope of seeing Marissa home and safe had crashed, and my mind and body were crashing now, too.

"There were some problems," Mom said, tugging off her jacket. She draped it over the back of the couch. "The wedding didn't happen." Her face crumpled. She looked about to start crying again.

Ada gasped. Her big round blue eyes went wide and she pressed a hand over her mouth. "Oh good Lord."

"I forgot the bags," Robby said. He turned and hurried out the front door to get them.

"Ada, do you think you could make me a cup of tea with lemon and bring it to my room?" Mom asked, her voice weak, just above a whisper.

Ada nodded and spun away, heading back down the hall toward the kitchen, her shoes clicking on the wood floor.

I checked my phone. No message from Dad. "Should I call Dad?" I asked. "See if anything has happened?"

But Mom was already halfway up the stairs. She didn't hear me.

I froze with my eyes on the stairway. I knew that Mom would have to pass Marissa's room to get to her bedroom. I hoped Marissa's door was closed. I hoped Mom wouldn't have to look into that silent, empty room.

Marissa, where are you?

Later, Robby was desperate to see Nikki.

"But I need the car to buy groceries," I said. "The fridge is completely empty."

"Can you drop me off?"

"Someone should stay with Mom," I said. "She really isn't doing well. Especially since Dad hasn't called."

"Mom is asleep," he said. "I peeked in on her a few minutes ago. Besides, Ada is here. I won't stay long, Harmony. Just drop me off at Nikki's, okay? You can pick me up on your way home from the grocery store."

Something about how desperate Robby was made me smile. True love. And for a moment, I had this sad feeling, realizing that I didn't have anyone I cared about as much as Robby cared about Nikki.

We climbed into Marissa's car. I sighed. The car smelled like Marissa. She loved this little car. . . .

I cruised through North Hills, our neighborhood, and turned onto Park Drive, which leads to Nikki's house near the high school. It was a warm, cloudy day, kind of damp, the air heavy, and droplets of drizzle dotted the windshield.

Robby cranked the radio up high and tapped his hands on the dashboard in time to the beat of some pop song. He's not into that music. I guessed he just put the radio on so we wouldn't have to talk about Marissa.

That was perfectly fine with me. I didn't feel like talking, either.

Nikki's family has a nice house on Kraft Avenue, a three-story brick home with a wide front lawn, and a tall evergreen hedge along the street. Robby clicked off the radio as I pulled into the paving stone driveway. He turned the rearview mirror to him and checked out his hair.

"You look stunning," I said sarcastically.

"Shut up," he muttered.

"How about *thanks* for driving you?"

"Thanks. I know it was a huge favor. I'll try to repay you someday." He can be sarcastic, too.

I stopped beside the front walk. He shoved open the door and leaped out of the car. He nearly tripped over one of the two round, white-painted stones that bordered the walk.

I shifted into reverse to back down the driveway. But I kept my foot on the brake and watched as the front door swung open before Robby reached the stoop.

Mrs. Parker, Nikki's mom, stepped into the doorway. She was dressed in tennis whites, a long-sleeved V-neck top and a short pleated skirt, and she had her platinum hair pulled back in a single braid beneath a white baseball cap.

"Hey, Mrs. Parker. I'm back. I came to see Nikki," Robby said, sounding a little breathless.

The passenger window was down, and I could hear every word.

Nikki's mom held on to the front door. "Oh, I'm sorry, Robby," she said. "You should have called. Nikki isn't here." She had a hoarse, scratchy voice. Robby told me she smokes a lot.

"But I *did* call," Robby protested. His words came out almost in a whine. He had his back turned to me, but I could imagine the disappointment on his face.

"It was a last-minute thing," Mrs. Parker said, still gripping the edge of the door.

"I . . . don't understand," Robby said. "What do you mean?"

She adjusted the cap over her hair. "Nikki went on a camping trip. With some other girls."

Robby scratched his hair. "Nikki? Camping? But she didn't tell me."

"Like I said, it was a last-minute thing."

Robby stood staring at her without moving. It was kind of an awkward moment. Like he didn't know what to say, and she just leaned there with the door half open.

"Oh. Nikki said to tell you not to call her." Mrs. Parker broke the silence.

"She *what*?" Robby turned, and I could see the alarm on his face.

"She said the phones don't work in the woods. No cell towers, I guess."

"Oh. Okay," Robby said softly. "Well . . ."

"She knew you'd be worried," Mrs. Parker added. "That why she said to tell you not to call."

Another long silence.

"When will she be home?" Robby asked.

Mrs. Parker shrugged. "Probably in two or three days. Depends on the weather, I guess." Raindrops began to patter the car windshield. "Sorry you came all the way over," she said.

"No problem," Robby replied. "My sister drove me." He motioned to the car.

Mrs. Parker waved at me. Then she nodded good-bye to Robby and closed the front door.

The rain was coming down pretty hard, but Robby didn't run back to the car. He sort of ambled, head down, hands in his jeans pockets. He slumped into the car, his face scrunched up, thinking hard.

"Roll up the window," I said. "It's raining hard. Or didn't you notice?"

"Nikki is not an outdoors person," he said. I couldn't tell if he was talking to me or to himself. "She hates the *idea* of camping. This is weird."

"Well . . . she's unpredictable," I said. "You have to admit she's unpredictable—bit of a wild card."

I backed down the drive and turned toward the Division Street Mall. "It's not your day, Robby," I said. "And now you'll have to come grocery shopping with me."

He groaned.

"It's a very short list," I said. "We can split it up and it'll take half the time."

He groaned again. He pulled his phone from his pocket.

"What are you doing?" I asked, pausing at a stop sign.

"Trying Nikki." He punched her number. One ring . . . two rings . . .

His phone was set loud. Even with it pressed tightly to his ear, I could hear clearly.

To his surprise, she answered on the third ring. "Hello?"

"Hey, Nikki. It's me," he said. "Where are you?"

I could hear her laugh. "Why do you keep asking me that? I told you before. I'm home."

THIRTY-FOUR

Robby blinked. He pulled the phone away from his ear, then pressed it back. "We have a bad connection," he told Nikki. "I thought I just heard you say you were home."

"But I *am* home," I heard Nikki reply. "Where else would I be, Robby?"

"But . . . I was just at your house," Robby told her.

I heard a loud click. "Nikki? Are you there? Nikki?" Robby cursed under his breath. "Lost her."

He pushed her number again. This time it went right to voice mail. He slammed the phone against the dashboard.

"Hey, don't have a fit," I said. "Take a breath. Count to ten."

He grabbed my arm. "Turn around. Turn the car around, Harmony."

I nearly sideswiped a parked SUV. "Are you serious?" I snapped. "Let go of me. I promised Mom I'd do the shopping."

"Go back," he insisted. "Go back to her house. I don't get this. I mean—"

"Okay, okay," I said. I switched the wipers on to high. The rain was coming down hard now, swept with strong gusts of wind. I clicked the headlights on. It was nearly as dark as night.

"I just don't get it," he repeated.

"Maybe she told her mom she was going camping and went to stay with a friend," I said.

"You mean another *guy*?" Robby's voice rose to the low roof of the car.

"No. I mean . . . well . . ." I realized I'd said a stupid thing. "Uh . . . maybe Nikki's mom got it wrong. Maybe Nikki plans to go camping *next* week or something."

Oh, God. Why didn't I just shut up? I wasn't helping the situation any. Robby pushed Nikki's number again on his phone and again it went straight to voice mail.

A truck sped by and sent a wave of water over my side of the car. I gripped the wheel tightly in both hands and turned onto Nikki's street. I saw a jagged bolt of lightning streak down in the distance.

I slowed as we drove onto Nikki's block. A black SUV was backing down her driveway. I recognized Mrs. Parker's white baseball cap and platinum hair. "Nikki's mom is leaving," I said.

"I've got eyes," Robby muttered.

I knew he was upset. Otherwise, I would have slugged him.

He jumped out before I stopped the car. Ducking his head against the rain, he ran onto the front stoop, splashed through a puddle at the top step, and pounded with his fist on the front door.

I watched from the car, the windshield wipers sending a steady beat as background music. I wanted the door to open. I wanted Nikki to be there. I wanted for Robby not to be disappointed. I wanted him to find out the truth.

Someone needed to find out the truth about *something*. Because I felt like we were all living in a world of total confusion, a world of no answers, no answers at all. It was exhausting. And more than that, I felt myself on the edge of tears, ready at all times to break out crying.

I could feel my emotions on the surface, feel the

prickling tension on my skin, all along my arms and legs, feel the tense tightness in my chest.

So I wanted Nikki to be there. I wanted *something* to have a happy ending.

But she wasn't there. Robby pounded the door and rang the bell, shoving his thumb down on it and pushing like he wanted to destroy it. He stood there, rain soaking his maroon hoodie, staring at the door as if he could will it to open.

But no. No Nikki. Nobody at all.

And he slumped back beside me in the car, closed the door, and sat there with his head down for a long time, his rain-drenched hair matted to his head.

"Why did she lie to me?" he asked finally. He wiped rainwater off his cheeks with one hand.

Again, I thought he might be talking to himself. But I answered anyway. "Who knows? Could be a dozen reasons. I don't want to hurt anyone's feelings, but you know she is a total flake."

He scowled. "You're so helpful. Thanks."

"Well . . . maybe she's in the woods somewhere like her mom said, and she doesn't want you to worry about her. She thinks you're still at the lodge. So she told you she was home."

He scowled some more. "Lame. Try again."

"Look. Maybe Nikki just . . . needed some space," I said. I shifted into reverse and started to back down the driveway. "You two have been all over each other. Maybe she was suffocating. Maybe she just needed to breathe."

"Wow. You suck at this," he said.

"I suck at what?"

"At cheering me up."

"Since when is that my job?" I could feel myself losing it. "Robby, we have a lot more important things to worry about than why Nikki lied about being home. Like our sister. Remember our sister? She's either lost or kidnapped or in hiding or out of her mind or dead or . . . or . . ." I was breathing too hard to continue.

"Okay, okay," Robbie said softly. "You're right. Of course." He turned away from me and stared at the raindrops sliding down the passenger window.

We drove home in silence, with the only sound the soft, steady scrape and squeak of the windshield wipers.

I dropped Robby home, then drove to the grocery store. The store was crowded—I guess people were stocking up for barbecues.

I was distracted. The fluorescent glare of the

overhead lights made me feel as if I were maneuvering my cart through a fog. I kept checking my phone, seeing if there was a message from Mom or Robby that they had heard from Dad back at the lodge.

The only message was from my friend Sophie, asking if I was back and did I want to come over and watch some movies or something on Netflix and order a pizza.

"Yes, I do," I murmured aloud. Something normal. Something to maybe keep me from wondering about Marissa for at least a few hours.

The checkout line was long. I grabbed a magazine off the rack to occupy my mind. But suddenly, a cold feeling gripped me. I felt a chill at the back of my neck.

Someone is watching me.

It was more than a feeling. It was as if I could feel someone's eyes on my skin.

I swung around, nearly knocking over the woman in line behind me. I saw quick movement a few aisles behind me. Someone darting out of sight?

I realized my heart was pounding. Was I imagining the whole thing? My mind was in such a total state of tension.

No. I had the cold tingling on my skin again. I turned back. No one there.

"Hey, miss—it's your turn," the woman behind me said, annoyed.

One last glance. No one there. I spun away and began to load my groceries onto the conveyor.

The rain had nearly stopped when I pulled up the driveway with a trunk full of groceries. To my surprise, Robby came hurrying out the kitchen door to help me carry them in. This was not like Robby at all. As I said before, he's allergic to helping out with pretty much anything. Maybe he felt guilty for the way he talked to me earlier in the car.

"How's Mom? Did you hear from Dad?" I asked, fumbling with the bags.

"Mom is a little better," he reported. "She's still in her room, but she isn't crying or anything."

He held the door open for me with his shoulder and I squeezed past him, my arms full. "And Dad? Did he call?"

"Yeah. But the news isn't really good."

"What do you mean?"

He lowered his bags to the kitchen counter. "There's still no sign of Marissa anywhere. And no clues, Dad said. The police are giving up their helicopter search."

I stopped to think. "That could be *good* news, you know. It means they didn't find her body at the bottom of the cliff." I pictured poor Taylor, her body crushed on the rocks, her pale face so still and empty.

Would I ever wipe her glassy stare from my mind?

"Yeah. Dad said the police are calling it a missing persons case," Robby said. He followed me back out to the car to retrieve the rest of the groceries.

I sighed. "How did Dad sound?"

"Mom talked to him. I didn't." He lifted out a light bag with bread and cereal boxes and left the heavy bag for me.

"Did he say he was coming home?" I asked.

Robby shook his head. "I think he's staying out there another day or two. You know. Just in case something turns up."

Marissa, where are you? Are you going to turn up?

I slammed the car trunk shut. A few drops of rain, swept down from the tree leaves, splashed my forehead. The cold made my skin tingle, and I shivered, more from my thoughts than from the water.

Sophie and I always have a good, giggling time together. She's seventeen like me, but she looks twelve. She's so short and skinny, and the big round-framed glasses she wears somehow make her face look babyish, and she has a little bit of a cartoon voice.

She's an awesome friend, and she lives three blocks from me, and we like the same movies and TV shows, and guys. I think Sophie disapproves a little of all the guys I've been with. But she's happy to take the overflow. Ha.

I feel guilty to admit it, given what has happened, but I always—since at least fourth grade—wished that Sophie was my sister instead of Marissa.

The rain had stopped. I pulled on Marissa's old red raincoat and walked to Sophie's house. The air felt cool and wet, refreshing on my hot face, and the lawns all sparkled under a bright half-moon. Two boys raced by on bikes, sending up splashes of water from deep puddles left by the rain. Somewhere down the block, two dogs were taking turns barking at each other, an intense conversation.

Normal life.

Sophie greeted me at the door with a story about a guy in our class who keeps texting her *hi* but then never responding after that.

I wanted to laugh about it and listen to her stories in her little cartoon voice, and tell stories of my own. But I realized as soon as the two of us were sprawled on pillows on the floor of her den that I couldn't have a normal night. There was *no way* I could just keep my story inside, push it away. I had to tell Sophie about Marissa and the nightmare at the lodge.

She listened openmouthed, her dark eyes bulging behind her big eyeglasses. And when I finished, she threw her arms around my shoulders and held me in a tight hug.

Then we stood there awkwardly. Both of us had tears in our eyes, and neither of us knew what to say next. But then Sophie's black Lab, Monroe, burst into the room, jumped up on me, and knocked me backward. I landed on my back on one of the big pillows on the floor, and the dog loomed over me and began licking my face.

"Stop! Stop!" I cried, laughing. Sophie pulled the dog away, but Monroe had succeeded in changing the mood.

We ordered a pizza and watched a funny old comedy on Netflix with Cameron Diaz and Ben Stiller, and we talked and laughed as if everything was okay, as if my family wasn't ruined, and my life wasn't crumbling.

We had a lot of fun, the way Sophie and I always do.

And nothing frightening happened to me until I walked home.

THIRTY-FIVE

"Call me as soon as you hear something," Sophie called from the front door as I made my way down her drive-way. "I've got all my fingers crossed that she's okay."

"Thanks," I shouted. I jumped around a wide puddle in the asphalt driveway. It had rained again while I was inside, and the air and the lawns and the whole world seemed to gleam and tingle in the dewy freshness.

The half-moon floated high in the sky, and it lit the roofs of houses all down the block. The windows were mostly dark. It was after midnight. But the houses seemed to shimmer in the still-wet air, and for a moment, I felt as if I were on a movie set. The whole scene couldn't be real.

It made me feel almost giddy. I guess I was on an

emotional roller coaster—sad and frightened because of Marissa, happy because of my fun night with Sophie. I felt alert and alive, as if I could see every blade of grass clearly, every star in the sky.

That feeling ended abruptly when I heard the first footstep behind me.

A soft splash, actually.

I stopped and listened. Silence now. I figured the wind had blown something down from the trees, something that splashed onto the sidewalk behind me.

But as I started to walk again, I heard a scrape and a soft thud that could only be a shoe on concrete.

I spun around and peered into the pool of darkness behind me.

No one there?

The tall trees cast deep shadows. I turned back, stepping into the dim yellow light of a streetlamp as I crossed the street.

My muscles were all tensed now. I realized I was clenching my jaw. I tried to step silently so I could hear the footsteps behind me clearly.

And yes, there they were. Running footsteps, picking up speed as I reached the other side of the street and began to trot.

But I wasn't fast enough. And a hand grabbed my shoulder roughly. And spun me around.

I screamed.

Then cut the scream short as I recognized my pursuer.

"Doug! What are you doing?" I cried.

His eyes went wide, and then he blinked several times, as if he was having trouble focusing. "Marissa—" he murmured.

I smelled beer on his breath. "Huh? Doug?" I said. "Are you okay?"

He didn't answer for a moment. He seemed to be struggling to keep his balance. His eyes were red-rimmed and his hair was wild and tangled. He shook his head. "Sorry, Harmony. I thought—"

He took an unsteady step back. "The red raincoat. I . . . thought you were Marissa."

"Oh, God," I murmured. I'd totally forgotten I was wearing my sister's raincoat. "Wow. Sorry, Doug."

"I didn't mean to scare you. I was just shocked. You know. I thought—"

I had a sudden thought. "Hey, Doug—were you in the supermarket this afternoon? Were you . . . watching me?"

He shrugged and lowered his eyes. "Yeah. Maybe. I didn't think you saw me."

"Why, Doug?" I asked. "Why were you following me? For news about Marissa? We . . . haven't heard from her."

I peered into his eyes, trying to read his mind. "I don't get it. Doug, *what are you doing out here*?"

He shrugged. Again, I got a whiff of the beer on his breath. "Just took a walk. You know. The rain stopped and I was bored, so . . ." His voice trailed off.

"We're all messed up about Marissa," I said. "The state police gave up their search. They say it's a missing persons case now. My dad is still out there." My voice caught in my throat. "It . . . it's just so hard not knowing if she's dead or alive."

Doug locked his eyes on mine. "She's alive," he said.

I gasped. "Huh? What do you mean?"

"She's alive, Harmony." He rocked unsteadily, then caught his balance.

I stared back at him, chills running down my back. "Doug—what are you saying? How do you know?"

He fumbled in his pocket and tugged out his phone. He raised it close to his face and, squinting hard at the screen, pushed the keyboard with his thumb. "Here.

Look," he said finally. "Look. It's a text message. It's from Marissa's phone."

"Are you serious?" I grabbed it out of his hand. I pulled the phone close to my face, and my hand trembled as I read the message, all in caps, just like the one in the note I found back at the lodge:

DON'T TRY TO FIND ME

THIRTY-SIX

The next day, Robby and I took Mom on a walk around the neighborhood. We *had* to get her out of the house. She had spent so much time in her room, not eating, not sleeping.

"She's aged ten years," I told Robby. "Look at her eyes. They're dead. And her hair. She barely brushes it."

"Dad has to get back here," Robby said. "What can you and I do?"

"Well, get her out of the house, for one thing."

It took a lot of convincing just to get her to take a short walk. "I don't want anyone to see me," she said. "I don't want to run into one of the neighbors and have to chat."

"I'll do all the chatting. I promise," I said.

It was a warm summer day, a few puffy white clouds high overhead, a soft breeze shaking the tree leaves. The kind of day that could make a person feel happy, if her sister wasn't missing and her family wasn't in shreds over it.

We made Mom walk five or six blocks. Robby and I tried to keep a conversation going, but it was pretty awkward. Mrs. Miller in the house on the corner waved from her front window, but we didn't run into anyone, and Mom didn't have to do any chatting.

When we got back to the house, the phone was ringing. Robby picked it up in the kitchen. I got Mom some cold water from the fridge.

Robby talked for a few minutes. He had his back turned, and I couldn't hear what he was saying. I leaned on the kitchen counter and waited for him to finish.

When he hung up, he turned to me. "Was that Nikki?" I asked.

He scowled at me. "Why would Nikki call on the landline? She'd call my phone."

"So who was that?" I asked.

"The police." He shook his head. "It wasn't good news."

I gasped. "What do you mean?"

"They have Doug's phone. They tried to trace the cell tower that text message came from."

"And?"

"And they couldn't trace it. They don't have a clue where it came from."

I sighed. "And they can't tell if Marissa really was the one who sent it?"

"Yeah. It says it was sent from her phone. But that doesn't really mean anything."

We stared at each other. The hum from the refrigerator suddenly grew louder. "Should we tell Mom?" I said finally. I glanced to the kitchen door. Mom was in the den. I knew she couldn't hear us.

"We didn't tell her about the text message, remember?" Robby said, leaning back against the cabinets. "We didn't want to upset her . . . without knowing . . ."

"We still don't know *anything*," I said, my voice cracking. "I'm seriously worried about Mom. She seemed so weak and fragile on our walk. She was always the strong one in the family."

"You can't blame her," he said.

"I'm not blaming her. I—"

"I'm totally messed up, too," he admitted. "We *all*

are, right? It's not like we can wake up one morning and say we can have a normal day today. A day without thinking nonstop about Marissa."

"I'm going to call Dad," I said. "I really think he needs to get home. For Mom."

Robby bumped me out of the way and pulled open the fridge. "What is there to eat? I'm totally starving."

I bumped him back. "Go get a bucket of chicken," I said. "I'm not in the mood to go grocery shopping again."

"Okay. I can get into that." He closed the fridge door. "Do you want regular or extra crispy?"

"Your choice," I said. "And don't forget the gravy for the mashed potatoes!"

He made a face at me. "I only did that *one time*, Harmony. So give me a break."

I laughed. It was one of the first normal conversations we'd had since before the wedding.

I told Mom we were having KFC for lunch. Then I walked down the hall to my room and closed my door. I sat down on the edge of my bed and raised my phone.

My good moment with Robby quickly faded from my memory, and I had a heavy feeling in my stomach as I prepared to call Dad. Dread. Total dread. It can make you feel heavy and cold.

The phone rang before I could dial, and I saw that it was a FaceTime call. I clicked *accept* and a second later stared at the face of my dad.

"Huh? I was just going to call you," I said.

"Well, I wanted to check in," he replied, "and see your face."

Of course, FaceTime makes everyone look weird because the camera is so close up. It's like a selfie, kind of distorted. But I could see that Dad looked tired. He hadn't shaved so he had a stubble of black beard over his cheeks with patches of gray. His eyes were only half open, as if he didn't have the energy to open them all the way.

"What's happening there, Harmony?" he asked. "How is your mother doing?"

"Not great," I said. "That's why I was going to call you. I think—"

The picture wobbled, then faded. A burst of static made me lower the phone. "Dad? Are you there?"

His face reappeared. I could hear the hum of voices in the background, someone shouting, and some kind of music playing.

"You disappeared for a second," I said. "Where are you?"

"I'm in the lobby," he said. "The Wi-Fi in my room is ridiculous." He jiggled his phone, and I could see the front desk of the lodge behind him.

"The police couldn't trace that text message," he said.

"Yes. They called here. Do you believe Marissa really sent it to Doug?"

He sighed. I could see his eyes begin to water. "I . . . I don't know *what* to believe, Harmony. I just don't. And I don't really know why I'm still here. I'm not doing any good. I mean, I'm not helping to find Marissa."

"Maybe you should come home, Dad," I said. "Maybe—"

And then I stopped, and a startled cry escaped my mouth.

Behind Dad in the lobby . . . I saw her. I saw the dark hair first and a blur of a face. Dad's phone slid to the right, and I saw her clearly. Right behind him.

Marissa.

Yes. Marissa. She was standing right behind him. On the screen, it looked as if she could rest her chin on the shoulder of Dad's polo shirt.

Marissa. She was there.

If only I could find the words. If only I could overcome

my shock and *speak*. Cry out. Shout to Dad. *Do something.*

"Dad—" I finally choked out. Marissa stared over Dad's shoulder, as if she could see me. She gazed into the phone. I could see her so clearly.

"Dad—" I couldn't get the words out. I couldn't make a sound.

"Dad—turn around!" I finally screamed. "Turn around! Hurry!"

PART FIVE

PART FIVE

THIRTY-SEVEN

Of course, by the time Dad turned around during our FaceTime talk, she had vanished. There was no one standing behind him.

"Dad—I saw her so clearly," I said, my voice trembling, my chest tight with emotion. "It was Marissa. I'm not crazy."

"The lobby is crowded," Dad said. Holding the phone unsteadily, he gazed all around. "You want to see her so badly, Harmony, you imagined that someone else was Marissa."

"No. No way," I insisted. "I know my own sister. Dad, she looked right at me. As if she could see me on your phone."

"Here. Look for yourself," he said. He turned the phone so I could see the lobby around him. I saw a woman with a baby stroller. Two teenagers with hockey sticks.

"Dad, I'm coming there," I said. "Please reserve a room for me. I'll be there as soon as I can."

The next morning, I flew to Boulder. Then I took a taxi from the airport, and we made our way up the sloping green hills to the lodge. The driver, a young guy with piercings all over his face, wanted to talk about baseball. He was a Dodgers fan.

I buried my face in my phone and hoped he would take the hint.

It was a sunny day up on the mesa, but windy. Gusts blew my hair straight up as I climbed out of the taxi, and my sweater fluttered around me like a flag or something.

Dad had reserved a room for me. I checked in at the front desk. Then I hurried to meet him. I had so much to tell him. The problem was where to begin.

Two girls about my age, both blond, passed me in the main hallway. They were both staring at the phones glued to their hands, white earbuds in their ears. I stared hard at them as they hurried by me.

I studied everyone I passed. I don't know what I

expected. Did I really think I'd just bump into Marissa in the hall?

I know she's here. I saw her.

I'll search from room to room if I have to.

Crazy idea.

The lodge café stood in an alcove halfway down the long hall. I stepped inside and waited for my eyes to adjust to the bright light.

Yellow afternoon sunlight filtered into the restaurant from three tall windows at one side. Black-and-white-checkered tablecloths covered the tables in the center of the room. Framed paintings of cows lined the walls. The whole place was light and bright and homey.

It was nearly two in the afternoon, and only a few tables were filled, people lingering over their coffee or dessert. I spotted Dad in a booth against the back wall. He waved and I trotted over to him.

We hugged and he kissed my cheek. "How was the trip?"

"Fine," I said. I slid across from him. I studied his face as I arranged myself and lowered the napkin to my lap. His eyes told the whole story. Dark circles around them and the eyelids red and puffy, as if he'd been crying. New wrinkles creased his forehead.

"Harmony . . ." He spun his water glass between his hands. "How are you holding up?"

I waited for the waitress to fill my water glass. Then I shrugged. "Okay, I guess. It's been hard."

"And how is your mother doing?"

"Not great." I had to be honest. "I think she really needs you at home."

He nodded. "So . . . are you going to ask me why I'm still here?"

"I don't know, Dad. I hadn't really planned—"

"Well, I don't really know why I'm still here," he interrupted. "It's like I'm holding on to something, I guess. I keep thinking maybe if I stay here, I'll be able to fix things. I mean, not fix things, but . . ." His voice trailed off.

"What can I get you?" The waitress loomed over the table.

Dad ordered a cheeseburger. I ordered a grilled cheese.

"You want chips or fries?" she asked.

I want my sister back.

"Chips," I said. I really wanted fries, but I was thinking too hard about everything else to say what I meant.

We watched her stride across the room to the kitchen.

I took a long sip of water. "Dad, I don't know where to start," I said. "I saw Marissa. I know you think I'm crazy, but I saw her standing behind you in the lobby."

"Harmony—"

I grabbed his hands and squeezed them. "Let me talk. I know it was her, okay. And I know when you turned around, there was no one there. But there's something strange going on here, Dad. In this lodge. Something that doesn't make any sense at all."

He sighed. "What *does* make sense?"

I told him about Walter the red-haired valet and Mr. Himuro at the front desk. I told him how I saw them and spoke to them when I saw Aiden arrive at the lodge. And how I couldn't find them later.

"They were in an old staff photo behind the front desk," I said, still gripping his hands. "A photo from 1924. But I talked to them, Dad. They were here."

I squeezed his hands. Mine were ice cold. I had the strange feeling that if I let go of his hands, I would lose him somehow. That the only way to get him to believe my crazy story was to hang on to him.

Dad blinked a few times. He didn't move. I felt his hands flinch under mine. I finally let go. I slumped back in the booth, breathless from telling my story.

I waited for him to speak, to react to my story. But he remained silent for a long while, and I could see his eyes narrow as he was thinking hard.

"You and I should both be locked up somewhere," he said finally.

I gasped. "Huh? What does *that* mean?"

"It means your story is crazy, and I actually think you're telling the truth."

"You believe me about Walter and Mr. Himuro. But you don't believe me about seeing Marissa?"

He fiddled with the collar of his blue polo shirt. "I want to believe you, Harmony. I want to believe everything. But it all just spins and spins in my mind. It's like the whole world is out of control, and only one thing remains true."

Across the room, I saw the waitress bringing our food on a tray. "What's that, Dad?" I asked. "What's the one thing?"

"That Marissa is gone."

I spent the afternoon hanging around the lobby, watching for Marissa. The lodge wasn't very crowded. July isn't a big month here. Most people come up for the skiing in the winter.

I sat in an armchair by the window and tried to concentrate on the Jane Austen book I'd brought with me. It was on the reading list for my senior Honors English, and I knew I would enjoy it if I didn't have to glance up every time someone passed by. Truth was, I couldn't concentrate at all, and the time slid by as if in a slow-motion haze.

I had come here for one thing only, and that was to find my sister, my sister who had gazed at me through Dad's phone yesterday, who had stood in this lobby, clear as day.

After a few hours, I'd read only twenty pages. Tired of sitting in one place, I left my perch and walked the long halls. I started on the first floor and covered all three floors. I didn't return to my room until the sun was lowering behind the trees.

Dad had some business things to take care of in town. I had a lonely room service dinner in my room. I texted Robby but he didn't reply. So I called Sophie, just to have some human contact, just to use my voice for a few minutes, to hear someone who lived in the real world and wasn't in this nightmare dream world of people appearing and mainly disappearing.

What time did I fall asleep? I guess it was early.

I was still in my clothes, and I just conked out with the TV on and the dinner tray still at the bottom of my bed, and the lights all on. I guess the stress of everything just wore me out, and I fell into a deep black dreamless sleep, sprawled on my back on top of the purple bedspread.

Such a deep sleep, I was surprised when the voices woke me.

At first, I didn't know where I was. I gazed up at the unfamiliar ceiling light, realizing I wasn't in my room at home. Then I recognized one of the *Real Housewives* shows on the TV, and saw my half-eaten dinner congealing on a tray at the bottom of my bed.

I'm at the lodge.

The voices broke into my consciousness. I heard them through the wall. Was it two women? Two girls? Their voices sounded young.

Were they arguing? I was still half in the heavy blackness of my sleep.

But I was startled completely alert when I recognized one of them. With a gasp, I jumped off the bed. Totally awake now, I hurtled to the wall and pressed my ear to the flowered wallpaper.

My head buzzed. I shut my eyes and concentrated. And listened to the voices in the next room.

"This isn't a good time. Listen to me."

"But I warned them. What more can I do? I don't want to hurt them."

"Do we have a choice?"

"If we stay hidden . . ."

I couldn't hear the rest of that sentence. But I definitely recognized the voice.

How could I not recognize my own sister's voice?

THIRTY-EIGHT

"Marissa!" I shouted her name. Then I spun away from the wall and lurched toward the door. Off balance because of my shock, I bumped the bed and sent the food tray crashing to the floor.

I jumped over the dinner plate, stumbled, caught my balance, and rocketed into the hall.

"Marissa! Marissa—it's me!"

I pounded my fist on the room next door. Room 258. My heart was pounding in my chest as hard as my fist on the door.

"Come on. Come ON! I heard you in there!" I shouted.

I pounded with both fists on the brown hardwood

door. "Marissa—open up! It's me, Harmony."

I held my breath, waiting for the door to open. But it didn't.

Silence.

I pressed my cheek against the door and listened. No voices now.

I wasn't asleep. I didn't dream them. I know they are in there.

"Open up, Marissa! I mean it! Open the door! I heard you! You can't hide in there. I *heard* you!"

Silence.

Two doors down, a door opened and a middle-aged man in a white bathrobe stuck his head out. "Is there a problem?"

"Uh . . . no," I said. "I . . . forgot my key. Just trying to get my sister to let me in."

"They'll give you another key at the front desk," he said, squinting at me in the bright hall light. "If she isn't there or something."

"Thanks," I said. *Great advice. Go mind your own business.*

He stepped back into his room and closed the door.

I raised my knuckles to the door and rapped a few more times.

"Come on, Marissa," I said in a low voice. "Open the door. I heard you, Marissa. Just open the door so I can see you."

Silence.

My fingers on both hands throbbed from my pounding. I was gasping for breath, wheezing, my chest heaving up and down.

I couldn't hold back the tears. I was so frustrated, I started to sob. I pressed my forehead against the room door and just let the tears come, and the sobs from deep in my chest. I cried so hard, it hurt.

"Marissa . . ."

And then I stopped crying as abruptly as I had started. I backed away from the door. I used the sleeve of my T-shirt to wipe my eyes and my tearstained cheeks.

The front desk.

That man had talked about going to the front desk.

I turned and gazed up and down the hall. No one out here but me. If I went to the front desk . . .

I knew I couldn't trick them into giving me a key to Marissa's room, room 258. But maybe . . . maybe I could trick them into opening the door for me.

I had an idea. An idea I knew would work.

Of course, I thought about casting a spell. Do you think I forgot all about my powers? The mischief I could do with the spells I learned from the old books in my attic?

I didn't forget. But I had learned how limited my skills were. And in hours of searching, I hadn't been able to find a spell to bring a vanished sister back. I couldn't even find a spell to *locate* a missing family member.

Yes, there was magic—dark magic—to bring the dead back to life. To summon the dead and talk with them. But those spells would take years to master. I could barely follow the complicated language that described them.

Besides, I didn't want to think about Marissa being dead. No. No way. She wasn't dead. She was just missing. And I was too inexperienced to deal with that powerful magic anyway.

And now here I stood trembling in the hall, and there was probably a fairly simple spell for opening a door. But I didn't know it. So my magic was useless.

I was useless.

But I'm pretty smart when it comes to getting people to do things for me. And I had a plan.

Marissa, I'm coming back. And I'm opening the door. I'm going to find you, Marissa. You cannot hide from me any longer.

I hurried down to the lobby. It must have been pretty late at night. The lights were dimmed, and the lobby was empty. Perched on a tall stool, a young man sat behind the front desk, concentrating on his phone. He wore a red-and-black flannel over jeans, and his light brown hair fell over his forehead.

When he saw me striding toward him, he took off his headphones and sat up straighter on the stool. "Can I help you?" He was probably twenty-one or twenty-two, but he had a very deep voice.

"I—I'm in room 256," I deliberately stammered. "And something is going on in the room next to mine."

He slid off the stool and set his phone down on the counter. "Like what?"

"I heard a girl screaming," I said. "Through the wall. It . . . it sounded scary. Like she was in trouble."

He brushed the hair off his forehead. "You mean—"

"She was screaming for help," I said. "Can you . . . send someone to check it out?"

He froze for a moment. He obviously hadn't dealt with many emergencies. He was the night clerk, and he was probably used to long, quiet, boring nights behind the desk.

He squeezed his phone, then pushed it across the desk. "Uh . . . What's the room number?" he asked finally.

"Next to mine," I said. "258." I bit my bottom lip and gave him my best frightened expression. "I think you'd better hurry. She sounded like she was in serious trouble."

He turned to the desktop computer beside him and tapped the keyboard, squinting at the screen. "Hmm . . . 258?"

I nodded. "Yes."

He squinted harder. Then he turned to me. "But that room is vacant. There's no one in there."

I uttered an exasperated sigh. "I know what I heard. I heard a girl screaming her head off in that room. Maybe someone forced her into that empty room."

That made him flinch. His mouth dropped open, but he kept his eyes on the screen. "It says here it's an empty room."

"Can we go see?" I asked. "We're wasting time here. Can't we take a look? Make sure a mistake hasn't been made? Maybe save a *life*?"

He peered down the long, dimly lit hall for some reason. "I'm the only one on duty . . ."

"Maybe we should call 911," I said. "Get the police here."

"No. I don't think so." He didn't like that idea. I figured he wouldn't want a bunch of cops barging in, waking up the guests.

He opened a drawer under the front desk and grabbed a key card. "Let's go."

We strode side by side down the main hall, then up the wide carpeted stairway to the second floor. I had to hurry to keep up with him. He was tall and thin, and he had long legs. He swung his arms as he walked, the key card gripped tightly in one hand.

"Do you know Mr. Himuro?" I asked as we made our way along the rooms on the second floor. I'm not sure why I asked. The question just popped out.

He shook his head. "I don't come on till nine. I don't know any of the day people."

We stopped in front of room 258. I struggled to catch my breath. Far down the hall, I heard a baby crying. The only sound except for the beating of my heart.

He tapped lightly on the door. "Hello? Anyone there?"

Silence.

He tapped again, a little harder.

I took a step behind him. I prepared myself for an emotional reunion with my sister. I mean, I couldn't really prepare myself. My muscles were all tight and knotted. I forced myself to breathe normally.

"Sorry to bother you," he called into the room. "This is the night clerk. Could you open up, please?"

He waited for a long time. It seemed like an hour or more. Then he turned to me. "You're sure?"

I nodded. I crossed my arms tightly in front of me.

"I heard her. I heard voices. In this room. I swear."

He raised the key card to the wall unit and clicked it. A little green light flashed on. He gripped the knob and slowly pushed open the door.

Dark inside. Still silent.

"Anyone here?" he called.

He fumbled on the wall and clicked a light switch. A lamp flashed on between two beds. The beds were made. I gazed all around the room, still hugging myself.

No sign that anyone had been there. Everything clean and orderly. Nothing out of place.

No sign. No people. No one.

It took me a while to realize that the night clerk was staring at me. "Did you have a nightmare?" he asked softly.

"Yes," I said. "A nightmare. I'm living a nightmare."

He clicked off the lamp. I followed him out of the room. I slid the door back, but I deliberately didn't close it all the way. I made sure it didn't lock.

I had a hunch. A stupid hunch. But, hey, I was about as desperate as a person can get.

I apologized at least six times to the guy. "No worries," he said, but I could tell he was suspicious of me. He definitely thought I was a lunatic. Maybe he was wondering if I could be dangerous. Ha.

He waited for me to dig my room key card out of my pocket and go into my room. I apologized again, then closed the door behind me. I heard him trotting down the hall.

I stood gazing out the window at the inky black sky. Now I didn't know what to do. I was wide awake. My heart was pounding. My skin tingled. How could I go back to sleep?

When I saw the white sheet of paper on my dresser top, it didn't register at first. I mean, I saw it but I didn't focus on it, and it didn't seem strange for it to be there.

But as my brain settled down, I realized I hadn't left a sheet of paper there. I uncrossed my arms and walked to the dresser. As I neared it, I could see the words in red ink across the page.

A note. It was a note of some kind.

I grabbed it and raised it into the light. And read the handwritten words:

DON'T TRY TO FIND ME

THIRTY-NINE

The note trembled in my hand. I lowered it to the dresser, leaned over it, and read the words again and again.

She was in my room. Marissa is here.

I knew that was her voice in the next room. I knew I heard her arguing with another young woman.

She was next door. How did she disappear before the night clerk and I opened her door? I didn't have a clue.

But here in front of me was proof that she was here in the lodge. And now that the coast was clear, what were the chances that my sister was right next door again?

Of course, there were crushing questions that weighed down my mind. Questions I didn't want to answer: Why was she avoiding me? Why didn't she want to be found? Why didn't she open the room door to me?

Why, why.

The questions led all the way back to: Why did she vanish on her wedding day?

And I knew the only way I'd ever get any answers was to find her and talk to her.

I stood over the dresser, staring at the words in red ink until they became a pink smear on the page. Then I shut my eyes tight and, clasping the dresser top, leaning over Marissa's note, I began to whisper the words of a spell. It was a simple spell I had easily memorized, a spell to make an object appear.

Almost like a magician's trick. Like making a dove suddenly appear in your hand. Yes, I knew Marissa wasn't an object. But this was the only appearance spell I could master.

I was desperate; desperate enough to try anything. I knew Marissa was close by. If only a simple spell would be enough . . .

I sank into myself, sank deep into my darkest corners, whispering the ancient words. When I finished, I opened my eyes. Nothing had changed.

What did I expect? That Marissa would be standing next to me?

It took a few seconds to get over my disappointment.

Then I turned to the door. And had a strong feeling . . .

Back in the hall, I stood on trembling legs in front of the door to room 258. I could see a thin line of light through the crack at the bottom of the door.

But the night clerk turned off the light. I could swear that he did.

And now the light was on.

I raised my fist to knock. Then I remembered that I hadn't closed the door all the way.

I grabbed the knob and, fighting the rapid humming-bird beats of my heart, slid the door open.

And uttered a startled cry. "I don't believe it!"

Marissa, sitting on the edge of one of the beds, turned, and her expression hardened. She didn't act surprised. The only emotion I could see was anger.

"I warned you, Harmony—" she said.

"Marissa! You're okay!" I cried, rushing across the room. "You're here! You're right here. I . . . I don't believe it!"

She stood up. She was wearing an outfit she always wore around the house—a maroon sweater over old black leggings. Her dark hair was tied back in a simple ponytail.

I threw my arms up to hug her. But I stopped when I saw the other two young women in the room. They both stood by the window. Both had their lips parted, eyes wide, watching me.

"Marissa—" I started.

She gestured to the two women. "This is my sister, Harmony," she told them. "Ruth-Ann and Rebecca."

I nodded a greeting.

"They're kind of cousins," Marissa said.

Ruth-Ann and Rebecca Fear? Why did their names seem vaguely familiar to me? My brain was swimming underwater. Staring at Marissa—actually here, actually in front of me—there was no way I could think straight about anything.

"You look a lot like your sister," Ruth-Ann said to me.

"Thank you," I said. Then I just stood there. I wanted to ask a thousand questions at once.

I gazed at the two Fear sisters. Ruth-Ann had short coppery hair. It came down just over her ears, with straight bangs across her forehead. Rebecca was prettier, softer-looking, with wavy straw-blond hair down past her shoulders and very large, light blue eyes.

They both wore long, flowery dresses, very silky and lacy, that came down nearly to the floor. Antique dresses, I realized. They must have been very expensive.

"I love your dresses," I blurted out. "They're antique, right?"

For some reason, both girls burst out laughing.

"Rebecca and I are antique, too," Ruth-Ann said.

And in that moment, I remembered.

I remembered the chapter about these two sisters in the book about the history of my family.

Rebecca and Ruth-Ann Fear, who both died at this lodge, who both plunged over the mesa rim . . . who died at Rebecca's wedding . . . in 1924.

I made a gasping sound as I remembered. And I felt my stomach lurch. I forced my dinner down. Held my hand over my mouth.

My knees folded. The shock was ringing through my whole body.

"Shut the door," Marissa said. "Sit down over there." She motioned to the armchair against the wall. "You might as well hear everything now . . . now that you found us."

I dropped into the chair. I pressed my hands over the soft leather arms. My hands were icy and wet.

"Marissa," I said, "I don't understand. These girls . . . they DIED!"

Ruth-Ann and Rebecca dropped onto the edge of the other bed.

"Yes. We died," Rebecca murmured, lowering her eyes.

I stared hard at her. She was so pretty. Like an angel, or a movie star from another time.

"But don't be scared," her sister added. "We're not ghosts who came back to haunt you."

They both giggled.

I turned back to Marissa. "Are you okay? You have no idea how worried we have all been. Worried isn't even the word. We have been *ruined* without you. All of us."

"I'm sorry," Marissa replied, lowering her eyes.

"Why are you here? Are you going to explain to me about these two? Will you explain *everything*?"

Marissa sighed and shifted her weight on the bed. "I didn't want to explain. That's why I left the notes. I can explain, Harmony, but you won't like it. Believe me. It's better not to know."

She stifled a sob at the end of her sentence. It was her first show of emotion.

"I *have* to know," I said. "Do you mean you're not coming home? You're not—"

Marissa turned to the other two. "Where should I start? Will it be too painful for you?"

Ruth-Ann frowned. "Painful? It's been too long since

I've felt anything as real as pain."

"Tell your sister the truth," Rebecca said. She straightened the folds of her long skirt, busywork for her fingers. "You really do not have a choice, Marissa."

"Tell me," I insisted. "Tell me." I hadn't realized I'd balled my hands into fists and I was waving them in front of me.

"You shouldn't be so eager," Marissa said to me. "There is no happy ending. I—"

"But, Marissa," I interrupted. "Don't you miss us? Don't you miss Mom and Dad? And Robby? Why did you run away? Why haven't you come home?"

"I can't come home, Harmony." Marissa's eyes watered but her expression didn't change. "Do you want an explanation or not?"

"Sorry," I said. I slid back in my chair and clasped my hands tightly together in my lap. "Sorry."

"You probably know their story," Marissa said, motioning with her head toward Ruth-Ann and Rebecca. "I know you read that book about our family's weird history."

"Rebecca's wedding," I said. "Yes. I read about it."

I glanced at her. She avoided my eyes. She stood up and walked to the window.

"Rebecca didn't know that the groom was a Goode. There is a curse on the Fear and Goode families. They can never marry."

I nodded. "Yes. I know about it. It was a long time ago."

"A long time," Rebecca said with great sadness. She peered out the window into the darkness of the mesa.

"Rebecca and Ruth-Ann were both killed that day," Marissa said, her voice steady but just above a whisper. I leaned forward in my chair to hear better. "Killed on what was supposed to be a joyful celebration."

She paused to wipe her eyes. Rebecca stood frozen, her back to me, gazing out the window. Ruth-Ann had her hands in her lap, her head bowed.

"It was a day of horror," Marissa continued. "A day of *too much* horror."

Ruth-Ann nodded. A sob escaped her throat. "Too much horror," she echoed.

"The horror was too much for anyone to bear," Marissa said. "Screams echoed off the mesa for hours. Wedding guests collapsed in sorrow. There were heart attacks. Two guests were paralyzed with strokes."

"Ohmigod," I murmured.

Marissa leaned toward me. "This will be hard for you to understand, Harmony. But the curse between the two families—the Fears and the Goodes—was much stronger than anyone realized. Rebecca had *married* Peter Goode. They kissed and the marriage was completed before he threw her over the cliff. A marriage the curse did not allow."

My mouth was suddenly dry as cotton. I realized I'd been holding my breath. I gripped the chair arms with my icy hands and waited for Marissa to continue.

"Minutes later, poor Ruth-Ann went over the cliff, too," she said in a voice just above a whisper. "But the curse would not allow the two sisters to rest. They were dead but they could not be at peace. The curse forced them to live on at this lodge—not growing older, not living a normal life or seeing anyone from their time."

Rebecca sighed. "Dead but not dead," she said.

"Alive in your time and in our time," her sister added, her eyes pleading with me to understand.

"They are trapped by the curse," Marissa said. "Some of the lodge workers were caught up in it, too. They cannot control when they live. They are sometimes in the past, sometimes here today."

"Walter the valet and Mr. Himuro . . . ," I muttered.

"They are caught in time, caught in the curse," Ruth-Ann said. "Like Rebecca and me."

"And now I am, too," Marissa said.

I uttered a cry. "What? What do you mean, Marissa?"

She shook her head. Her face drooped in sadness. Again, tears filled her eyes. "This is the part I didn't want you to know, Harmony."

"What?" I demanded, fearing the answer.

"I'm dead, too," Marissa said. "Killed on my wedding day."

"NOOOOOO!" I wailed, leaping to my feet. "No! It can't be true. Please—say it isn't true."

She moved forward and wrapped me in a hug. "I'm so sorry. So sorry. But I'm dead, too, dear."

"Who?" I cried, pressing my cheek against hers. "Who did it, Marissa? Who killed you?"

"Aiden killed me," she whispered.

FORTY

The shock of Marissa's words made my whole body shudder. A horrified cry burst from deep in my chest. I staggered back and sat on the edge of the armchair, struggling to catch my breath.

"Aiden?" The name slipped from my mouth.

"He's here with Nikki," she said. "A double surprise. I had no idea the two of them were together."

I stared back at her. My head was spinning. This was all too much, too much to take in at once. My heart throbbed. I had red flashes in my eyes.

"Aiden and Nikki have been together ever since that night I brought Aiden home to our house," Marissa said. "Remember? Nikki jumped into Aiden's lap, just to be funny? Something happened between them, I guess. Like lust at first sight. Ha."

She shook her head. "Of course, I didn't know it till now, till Aiden just explained it to me."

Her eyes suddenly had a faraway look, as if she was no longer looking at me but seeing the past.

I squeezed the arms of the chair. "But . . . Robby," I uttered. "What about Robby?"

Marissa made a disgusted face. "Nikki said she was never into Robby. It was mean, but she was just having fun, playing with him, making a fool of him. He never knew what was going on. None of us did."

She shook her head. "None of us knew what a liar Nikki is. She told her mother she went on a camping trip with friends. But instead, she came here with Aiden."

Marissa shifted again on the bed. "Of course, Aiden *loved* stealing Robby's girlfriend."

I blinked. "Because . . ."

"Because Aiden *hates* us," Marissa snapped. "And don't give me that innocent face, Harmony. It's all your fault that he hates us, and you know it."

Her sudden anger made my heart start to pound. I could feel my face turn hot, and I knew I was probably beet red. "But—"

"You ruined his life, Harmony," Marissa continued.

"Aiden dreamed of being a surgeon since he was a little kid. And you ruined it. You destroyed his dream. So . . . he decided to destroy our family."

"Huh? By stealing Robby's girlfriend?" I cried.

Marissa shook her head. "No. By murdering me. He killed me, Harmony. He threw me over the cliff."

"No—" I gasped. "This is impossible. You—"

"Taylor and I went up on the mesa early on the morning of my wedding. We went up to watch the sunrise. Aiden showed up. He showed us how he still can't use his hand. He said our family had to pay. He was crazed. He was totally psycho. Then . . . Then . . ."

She took a breath. "Then he rushed at me. Lowered his shoulder and plowed into me. I begged him. I *begged* him. But he knocked me backward. Shoved me like a mad bull. Knocked me over . . . over the cliff. He killed me."

Marissa was gasping for breath now, her whole body heaving up and down. "Taylor tried to save me. She dove at Aiden. Tried to tackle him. But she missed and went sailing over the edge."

"They found Taylor's body," I said, my voice breaking. "Poor Taylor. Why isn't she here with you, Marissa? Why isn't she here like you three?"

"She isn't a Fear," Marissa replied. "The curse had

no hold over her." A sob escaped her throat. "She was such a sweet, sweet friend. I hope she rests in peace."

"Unlike us," Ruth-Ann murmured bitterly.

"But . . . here's the frightening part," Marissa said, locking her eyes on mine. "Aiden took his revenge on Robby by stealing Nikki. He took his revenge on me by murdering me. But . . . what does he plan to do to you?"

A chill ran down my back.

Before I had a chance to react, the door to the room crashed open. It slammed hard against the wall. I jumped to my feet as Aiden burst into the room.

Aiden wore a navy-blue shirt, untucked, sleeves rolled up, over baggy black jeans, ragged holes at both knees. "Wow. The Fear girls are reunited," he said, a strange smile on his face, his eyes gleaming, hair falling over his forehead. "Harmony, you found your sister."

I opened my mouth to reply, but no words came out. I gaped at him in shock. "You . . . you're still here?" I finally choked out. "But—how?"

"I don't know," Aiden said, moving closer. "I keep moving between two times. It's like I'm trapped. Maybe it's just more of my bad luck, my ruined life. Just something else I can't control or even understand. But . . . I have some unfinished business, Harmony."

I uttered a cry as he grabbed my arm. "You want to

stay with your sister, right?" He brought his face close to mine and spit the words. "You want to join her, right?"

"Let go of me," I cried. I twisted my arm out of his grasp, but he quickly grabbed it back.

"Ow. You're hurting me," I said. "Let go, Aiden—" I struggled to pull away, but his grip was surprisingly strong.

He reached into his jeans pocket with his other hand and pulled up a gleaming object. I watched it glow as he raised it, and it took me a few seconds to realize I was staring at a knife blade.

"N-no—!" I stammered a choked protest.

Aiden wrapped his arm around me, holding me against him. "It's a surgical knife," he said. "My father's first surgical knife. He always planned to pass it down as a memento to me when I became a surgeon. But . . . that isn't going to happen, *is* it, Harmony?"

"Let her go," Ruth-Ann shouted. "Aiden—don't do this."

He glanced back at Ruth-Ann. "Harmony wants to be with Marissa. She wants to stay with her beautiful sister."

He tightened his grip on me and raised the knife in front of my eyes. I twisted and squirmed, but my terror was weakening me. I could feel the panic freeze my body.

"There's only one way to join Marissa," Aiden said, his hot breath brushing my ear. "You have to die."

He pressed the blade against my neck. And slid it slowly across my throat.

FORTY-ONE

The blade felt warm against my skin. I started to gag.

Aiden laughed and lowered the knife. "Too messy," he said. "Cutting your throat would be too messy, Harmony. I just wanted to give you a thrill."

"Let go of me!" I screamed. "You're *crazy*!"

Marissa stepped up to Aiden. "Let go of her. You've already had your revenge."

"Harmony wants to be with you," he said, tightening his grip on me, bending me backward. "She wants to be with her beautiful cousins over there."

"Let go! Let go!" I screamed, panic choking my throat.

"It only hurts for a few seconds," he said. "When

you fall off the cliff, it only hurts when you land. And then . . ."

"No, Aiden. Don't do it," Marissa pleaded. She grabbed his arm. "Don't do it."

"Listen to her," I heard Rebecca say.

The last words I heard before everything went black.

I blinked my eyes open, then shut them. My head didn't feel like a human head. It felt like a rock of throbbing pain.

I groaned. "Where am I?"

I opened my eyes again. A shadow rolled over me. A face peered down, studying me. Aiden.

"Get up," he ordered. He grabbed me roughly by one arm and tugged me to my feet.

The ground tilted and spun in front of me. My eyes refused to focus. Blurs of colored light danced around me.

"Aiden—?" I choked out.

Then the tall grass came into focus. The dirt leading up to the flat edge of the rock cliff. Slowly, my brain rolled over, regained some ability to think, to remember, and I knew I was high on the mesa, just a few feet from the cliff edge.

"No—Aiden!" I heard Marissa's desperate cry.

"Aiden—don't!" A plea from Ruth-Ann. I saw her lingering back in the grass, huddled with her sister and Marissa.

The ground still swirled beneath me. My head spun and throbbed. I struggled to come back all the way, but the blow on the head had me woozy and weak.

Aiden gripped me by both shoulders. He gave me a hard push. "Over you go, Harmony, sweetheart." He spit the words in my ear. "You won't ruin any more lives."

Another hard shove.

One more shove and I knew I'd be over the edge. I'd be gone. Dead. Maybe trapped in time here forever, or maybe lost like poor Taylor.

One more shove . . .

I lowered my gaze and saw the ragged floor of gray-brown rocks far below. The sight made me gasp. My brain whirred into action.

One more shove . . .

The words of a spell ran through my frightened brain. A darkness spell? I didn't know it well enough. Would a deafening blast of sound be enough to make Aiden let go of me so I could flee?

The dirt at the cliff edge crumbled under my shoes. Aiden tightened his fingers on my shoulders, about to give me the last push.

I shouted out the words of a spell I knew, shouted them to the sky.

I felt Aiden's fingers loosen, his hands pull away.

He uttered a startled cry—and did a wild cartwheel—up high in the air, twisting his body. As he flipped over, his hands touched the edge of the cliff, and then he sailed over the side.

His scream sounded like the wail of a wounded animal.

I left him suspended in air. Screaming in air. I controlled him with my eyes, muttering the words of the ancient magic. He was head down, still in the grip of his cartwheel, hanging in midair.

What shall I do with him? Why not just leave him there?

Then with Aiden's screams in my ears, I turned and ran, ran past Marissa and the Fear sisters . . . ran down the dirt path to the lodge.

Still dizzy, still reeling from all the horror, I zigged and zagged and staggered through the front entrance. And prayed . . .

Please . . . please let it be today and not the past.

Yes!

The young woman behind the desk cried out and

jumped off her chair as I dove over the counter. I landed hard on my elbows and knees. Scrambled to my feet.

"What are you doing? Somebody—help me!" she screamed.

I turned to the wall, struggling to catch my breath— and grabbed the frame of the 1924 photo in both hands. With a wrenching swipe, I pulled it off the wall.

"Stop her! Somebody—stop her!" the poor, alarmed girl wailed. She backed away from me, shouting for help.

"Don't worry," I choked out. "Don't be scared."

I tore the back of the frame away and tossed it on the floor. Then I pulled out the old photo. The paper was stiff and crinkly. The photo smelled old, kind of sour. I pressed it to my forehead.

Yes, I pressed the photo to my forehead. Shut my eyes. And murmured the words I'd seen in one of the old books of Fear magic. Murmured the words I'd memorized, I was so entranced by this spell.

I'd never gotten it to work. But this time . . . this time . . .

I murmured the words until the desk clerk's screams faded from my ears. Pressed the old photo to my head and repeated them again and again.

This time . . . this time . . . it had to work.

FORTY-TWO

The buzzing in my ears grew louder . . . louder . . . then started to fade. I felt a powerful shock wave, like a strong current that shook my body and took my breath away.

And when I lowered the photograph from my face and blinked my eyes open in the yellow-white sunlight, I saw the men in their dark suits, lined up in front of the lodge entrance. Square black cars in the driveway, like cars from a silent movie.

And the chubby, dark-suited photographer leaning over his big square camera, adjusting the tripod, gazing into a round lens, his jacket open and flapping in a strong summer wind.

I squinted hard and recognized Mr. Himuro in the

front row, and behind him, having a mock fistfight with the lodge worker next to him, Walter the valet, his red hair slicked back and glowing in the warm sunlight.

Yes. I had achieved it this time. I was in 1924. Thanks to the magic I had learned, thanks to the hours I'd spent practicing in that little attic room.

I was in 1924, where I wanted to be. And I went running toward the two men on the lodge staff that I knew. Perhaps one of them could help me.

Whoa. I stopped a few feet from them as the photographer counted down. "Three . . . two . . . one . . ." And he snapped his photograph with a powdery flash of bright light.

I suddenly realized I was no longer holding the photograph. It had vanished. Vanished into time, I guessed, since the photographer had just snapped it.

The workers were heading back to the lodge. I ran up to Mr. Himuro. I startled him by grabbing his arm. "Mr. Himuro, do you remember me? I need a favor."

He squinted at me, studying me as if I were a species from another planet. I guessed my clothes were shocking to him, or perhaps my long hair. "So sorry," he said. "I have no time. There is a big wedding here in a few hours."

I turned and raised my eyes to the mesa. I could see rows of white chairs up near the top, and an altar covered in purple flowers.

"The Fear wedding?" I asked him.

He nodded and hurried away.

"The Fear wedding," I repeated. Rebecca Fear's wedding. I was in time. I knew what I had to do. It was simple. I had to break the curse.

The silky long dresses were so wonderful. Everyone so dressed up, the men in their dark suits and stiff-collared shirts and wide neckties. The women clanking with jewelry, heavy bracelets and jeweled beads, and such awesome old-fashioned hairstyles. I felt as if I were in an old movie, only in color and with sound.

I stayed in the back row. Even back here, I could sense the excitement. The buzz of voices . . . the crinkle of fabric as the wedding guests seated themselves . . . the heavy perfume that filled the air, so intoxicating.

Then the music started and a hush fell over the seats. And I tensed every muscle. I steeled myself for what I had to do. I forced my heartbeats to slow. Forced down the waves of nausea from the pit of my stomach. Leaned forward and prepared myself.

Doing his processional slow walk, the groom made his way past me toward the flower-covered altar. Peter Goodman. Peter Goode. Peter Goode here to keep the old family curse alive. Peter Goode, not Goodman. If he was allowed to triumph, the Fear girls—from now and the future—would be doomed.

Rebecca, lovely Rebecca and Ruth-Ann, and my sister, Marissa. Their names were in my mind and in my heart as I watched Peter Goode's best man follow him along the aisle.

And I bit my bottom lip and clasped my hands tightly in my lap when Rebecca, the bride, made her journey down the aisle, smiling so broadly at her soon-to-be husband.

Only not.

You didn't know you were walking to your death, Rebecca.

Can I save you?

Maybe.

I waited. I don't know how I found the strength to wait. I wanted to have it over with. I wanted to know if I could save the three Fear girls . . . stop the curse . . . save everyone.

The ceremony began. I could hear only a mumble of

voices from here in the very back. The minister droned on for a while, something about "the sanctity of marriage." Whatever that means.

I waited.

A little boy in a black tux near the front kept repeating loudly, "I want ice cream." His dad grabbed his arm, shook him a little, trying to quiet him.

A burst of wind sent Rebecca's veil flying like a flag behind her head. Her hair was up like a golden crown.

I waited.

And then I knew the words were coming. And I knew I had to act before I heard the words *You may now kiss the bride.*

Before the kiss could take place . . . before the fatal kiss . . . I began to whisper the words of the spell, the spell I'd so recently practiced.

I whispered the words rapidly, so eager now to end the curse . . . to prevent the murders.

I had nearly completed it . . . I knew I could do it. I knew I could send Peter Goode cartwheeling over the cliff edge. . . . Yes . . . Yes . . . Good-bye, Peter Goode.

I was on the final words—

—when someone grabbed my arm—and started to pull me off my chair.

FORTY-THREE

"Let go—!" I gasped.

I stared at the little boy in his shiny tuxedo. He tugged my arm again. "Ice cream," he said. "Can you get me some ice cream?"

I turned to the altar and saw Peter Goode lift Rebecca off her feet. Guests oohed and aahed, touched by his romantic gesture. But I knew the truth. I knew he had murder on his mind.

If he kissed her . . . If he kissed her, all was lost.

"Later," I told the kid. "Later. Okay?" I jerked free from his grasp. I jumped to my feet and shouted the last words of my spell.

A hush fell over the mesa as Peter set Rebecca back

down on the ground. Without a kiss. No kiss! Peter turned to the cliff and raised his hands high above his head.

And performed a perfect cartwheel into the air and off the cliff. A perfect cartwheel to his death.

And now the silence was broken by cries of horror and moans of disbelief. People fainted and grabbed their chests and turned away, too late—too late because the horrifying scene was already imprinted in their minds and eyes.

Rebecca collapsed to her knees, covering her face as she sobbed, her veil falling over her head like a shield.

She was sad and shocked, I knew. But she was alive. And Ruth-Ann would continue to live. And my sister . . . My sister would live, too, and not be caught in the Fear family curse.

I had broken the curse. . . .

As I gazed over the scene, the color began to fade to shades of gray and black. The heavy-sweet aroma of the perfume faded. The sunlight dimmed, and the wedding guests all vanished. Rebecca and Ruth-Ann, her parents, her guests . . . all vanished into time.

And now nearly one hundred years passed. And here I was at the lodge on the day of my sister's wedding. How eager was I to knock on her door after breakfast and ask if I could help get her ready.

She flung her door open and wrapped me in an excited hug. And for a moment, I thought she was hugging me because she knew I had saved her life.

But of course she was just feeling exuberant and loving and excited on her wedding day.

"You look beautiful already," I told her. I saw that Taylor was waiting to help with her dress. "Is there anything I can do?" I asked.

Marissa nodded. "There are some packages for me at the front desk. Could you get them?"

Of course. Can I describe how happy I was at this new reality, this happy reality where Marissa didn't die and disappear? I don't think I can.

I waited at the front desk as a couple with two noisy, arguing kids checked in. A valet came to take their bags to their room.

"I believe you have some packages for my sister," I said. I recognized Lisa, the young woman on duty.

"Yes, I do," she said. Then she stopped. And squinted at me. "Hey," she said.

"What's wrong?" I asked.

She moved to the wall and stopped in front of the framed photo from 1924. "Look," she said, and pointed.

"This girl in the old photo. You look just like her."

"Huh? That's crazy," I said. I leaned over the counter and studied the photo. And yes, there I was, standing by the gathering of workers in 1924.

"You really look like her," Lisa said. "You're like twins."

"Weird," I said. "That's totally weird."